The Book of Shadows

Also by C.L. Grace

The Merchant of Death

The Eye of God

A Shrine of Murders

'Gentlemen, think, there has been war of old
In every class waged between men and gold,
So strong there's almost any to be had.
Alchemy has made many people mad.'

—Geoffrey Chaucer

'The Canon's Yeoman's Tale'

In the Middle Ages women doctors continued to practise
in the midst of wars and epidemics as they always had, for the simple
reason that they were needed.

—Kate Campbellton Hurd-Mead

A History of Women in Medicine

The **Book of Shadows**

(Being the Fourth of the Canterbury Tales
of Kathryn Swinbrooke, Leech and
Physician)

C. L. Grace

St. Martin's Press ⚮ New York

Library of Congress Cataloging-in-Publication Data

Grace, C. L.
    The book of shadows / by C. L. Grace.
        p.   cm.
    ISBN 0-312-14287-0
    1. Swinbrooke, Kathryn (Fictitious character)—Fiction.   2. Great
Britain—History—Lancaster and York, 1399–1485—Fiction.
    3. Women physicians—England—Canterbury—Fiction.   4. Women
detectives—England—Canterbury—Fiction.   5. Canterbury
(England)—Fiction.   I. Title.
PR6054.O37B66   1996
823'.914—dc20
                                                                    96-2439
                                                                        CIP

First Edition: June 1996

10 9 8 7 6 5 4 3 2 1

To a great scholar of Canterbury, Dr. William Urry: Many thanks

Historical Note

By summer 1471 the bloody civil war between the Houses of York and Lancaster had ended with Edward of York's victory at Tewkesbury. The Lancastrian king, Henry VI, was quietly murdered in the Tower. Edward IV with his beautiful wife Elizabeth Woodville and their gangs of henchmen now controlled the kingdom. Nevertheless, the Civil War had left bitter memories: old grudges and scandals died hard. Grievances were recalled and scores settled; this was fertile ground for the professional blackmailers who flourished as vigorously then as they do now.

The Book of Shadows

Prologue

Tenebrae, the great magus or warlock, sat in his velveteen-draped chamber in his house on Black Griffin Lane. Although within walking distance of many churches and the Priory of the Friars of the Sack, Tenebrae was not interested in the religion practised by the good citizens and burgesses of Canterbury. Not for him the Mass, the body and blood of Christ elevated by the priest before the crucifix. Nor would Tenebrae join those devout pilgrims who, now spring had come, flooded into Canterbury. They would make their way to the great cathedral to mount the steps on their knees to the Lady Chapel and pray before the bliss-ful bones of Saint Thomas à Becket.

Tenebrae believed in other, darker gods. His world was filled with goblins and sprites, for he had carefully studied the secret lore of the ancients. Tenebrae lifted the mask from his smooth, shaven face and peered around. All was dark. He preferred it that way. Ever since he was a child, skulking in the alleys of Cheapside in London, Tenebrae preferred the shadows, hence his name. He did not want to feel the sun nor did he want others to look on his face with its cloven lip and balding dome, or those eyes, which frightened children and chilled the heart of those who caught his gaze. Light blue they were, like slivers of ice, ill-matching in the soft, creamy folds of his hairless face. Tenebrae shifted his dark cloak on which pentancles and other signs of the zodiac were sewn. He heard a sound and his head rolled round, scrutinising the long chamber carefully. Everything was in order. The two doors, the entrance and the exit, which only could be opened from the inside, were firmly closed and locked. In the light of the solitary candle, which was fashioned out of wax and contained the fat of a hanged man, the floorboards, painted a glossy black, gleamed and shimmered. The velvet drapes on the wall hung solid. Tenebrae stared up at the ceiling and studied carefully the picture of the goat of Mendes, red and garish, with terrible horns and the gleaming eyes of a panther.

Tenebrae pronounced himself satisfied but he remained seated, cross-legged in the middle of the magic circle he had drawn. He opened the Book of Shadows, the grimoire of Honorius, that great magician of Roman times. The book was bound in human skin, ornamented with red gemstones and demonic seals and, when shut fast, held secure by clasps fashioned out of the skull of a lapwing. Tenebrae studied the yellowing pages and the strange cramped writing. He leaned over and pulled the great candlestick closer. He smiled, a mere puckering of his strange lips; then the smile died. He paused in his reading as he heard a sound from the street pilgrims thronging below.

'Fools,' he murmured.

He stroked the pages of the grimoire: here was true knowledge!

He spoke to the darkness. 'Why go and pray in front of a sarcophagus containing mouldy bones or pay good silver to gaze in awe at the rags of some mouldering monk three hundred years dead?'

Tenebrae recalled his mother, her devout mumblings, her constant visits to churches and faithful obedience to priests. Much good it did her, Tenebrae reflected. She had died of the plague and her son, left to his own devices, had been drawn into darker circles. He had become a student greedy for the ancient knowledge, ambitious to become a Lord of the Crossroads, a magus, a warlock. Had he not studied the secret knowledge of the Templars and gone to Spain to divine the mysteries of the Cabala? And then to Rome and, finally, Paris where, by skill and sheer ruthlessness, he had become a Great Master of the coven and the proud possessor of the grimoire of Honorius.

Tenebrae touched the broad platter before him: a black cock lay there, its throat severed, a bundle of pathetic feathers as its life-blood poured out into the gold-encrusted bowl Tenebrae had held beneath its neck. The magus had made his prayers to the Great Lord. He had fasted for three days to prepare his powers, to ask protection. Tenebrae was no charlatan. He did not indulge in conjuring tricks. Could he not fill a house with the intangible darkness? Had he not in his own private temple summoned up, at least in his mind's eye, all forms of terrible spirits? Great devils in the shapes of horses with men's faces, lions' teeth and hair like writhing serpents, crowned with circlets of gold, armoured with breastplates of cruel barbed iron? Tenebrae ran his tongue over his blackening teeth. Had not the Archbishop of Toulouse said that around every great magus demons gathered, a thousand on the right, ten thousand on the left? And had not the same cleric reckoned that over 133 million angels had fallen with Lucifer from heaven? Tenebrae closed his eyes and began slowly to chant his praises to these secret, dark lords. He closed the grimoire and, picking it up, stroked it carefully. Tomorrow he would be busy. The pilgrims would flock to the cathedral but there were others who would come secretly here to have consultations with him. Everything was ready: the stool where his visitors would sit was placed before the great table and, behind it, his throne-like chair. Tenebrae would scatter the bones and draw aside the curtains of the future, his visitors would pay good gold for that. Some, the great ones, would even pay more because Tenebrae was no fool.

There were those high in the church who would like him investigated, arrested, put on trial for witchcraft. Tenebrae grinned; they dare not. The magus had discovered how the powerful have two weaknesses: their ambition for the future and their secrets from the past. Tenebrae always found the latter most useful. He had a network of friends and acquaintances, tittler-tattlers at court, hangers-on, gossip collectors from the Great Council. Tenebrae would listen to these carefully, pore over this letter, study a manuscript, sniff like some good hunting dog until the juicy morsels of scandal were dragged out. The magus would then salt it away in his prodigious memory until he needed it, either for his own protection or greater profit.

Indeed, Tenebrae's sacrifice this morning was an act of thanksgiving for the years that had been good to him. The civil wars between York and Lancaster had led to the revelation of many secrets and scandals. Now that the House of York was in ascendancy, and golden-haired Edward IV sat on the throne at Westminster, there were many nobles and merchants eager to conceal which side they had supported in the recent civil war. Alongside these were bishops and priests, eager for enhancement, who had broken their vows and the sanctity of their lives in order to outdo a rival. There were retainers who had betrayed their masters, noble wives who had cuckolded their husbands.

Tenebrae had listened, sifting through all this information as a good apothecary would herbs and potions. The magus pursed his lips in satisfaction. And so who could touch him? Did not even Elizabeth Woodville, Edward IV's queen, consult him? Had she not called on Tenebrae's powers to achieve what she wanted? Offering her white, satin body to the King so she could master him in bed and thus control the Crown of England. In helping her, Tenebrae had found out a lot more about Elizabeth Woodville and her husband.

The magus got to his feet, his bulky body swaying as like some priest with his breviary, he clasped the grimoire to his chest. This was not only a Book of Shadows, but the keeper of secrets. He tapped the gold bowl with his foot and stared down at the rich, dark red juice congealing there. He would clear the room and, tonight, break his fast on roast swan, carp cooked in spicy sauces and goblets of wine. Tomorrow he would return here with his visitors, open the Book of Shadows, predict the future, hint at the past and spin gold for himself.

Elizabeth Woodville, Queen of England, rested in the pleasaunce, which her husband the King had specially built for her in the lee of a small hill, which ran down from the palace of Sheen to the Thames. Elizabeth sat back in the small, flower-covered arbour; the sun was unexpectedly strong and Elizabeth prided herself on the whiteness of her skin. 'My Silver Rose!' her hot-blooded husband Edward whispered in her ear. 'My jewel of great price!' Elizabeth pulled down the white gauze veil in front of her eyes and carefully stroked the sheer satin of her tawny dress. Behind her, on a garden seat, she could hear her ladies-in-waiting giggling and whispering around the royal nurse holding baby Edward, her eldest son: Elizabeth's final clasp over the affections of her husband. The Queen studied the swans swimming serenely along the Thames like galleys of state. She admired the curve of their necks, the sheer majesty of these great birds and recalled Edward's promise that the appointment of a keeper of the swans was within her power.

Elizabeth smiled and put her head back against the cushioned wall. Indeed, she had all the power in the realm. Edward the King ruled England and she ruled Edward. Perhaps not in public when Edward sat enthroned but, in the boudoir, between the sheets of their great four-poster bed, Edward was her slave and Elizabeth was determined to keep things that way. A year had passed since the end of the civil war and she had come out of sanctuary in Westminster Abbey to receive the adulation of the crowd and the loving embraces of her husband. Henry VI, the old Lancastrian king, was dead, his skull cloven in two whilst the holy fool prayed in his death chamber in the Tower of London. All the Lancastrians were dead, except for thin-faced Henry Tudor, but he was a mere shadow against her sun.

Beneath her gauze veil Elizabeth's face hardened. The present and the future held no terrors for her. But the past? The Queen chewed on carmine painted lips, her amber-coloured eyes snapping in anger. In matters of war and statecraft, Edward of England was as magnificent as he was in bed, but in the affairs of the heart, he was indiscreet. Elizabeth had her secrets and so did the King; the Queen was now determined to discover what these secrets were whilst keeping a firm grip on those matters she wished to hide.

'What does Tenebrae know?' she murmured.

Elizabeth recalled the pasty white face of the great necromancer. Those blue eyes, so light they gave his gaze a milky look like that of some old, blind but dangerous cat Elizabeth had glimpsed in the Tower menagerie. She stirred restlessly, picked up the jewel-encrusted goblet of hippocras and sipped carefully.

'Your Grace!'

Elizabeth lifted her gauze veil and smiled brilliantly at the young man who had appeared so silently in front of her.

'Good morning, Theobald. I was thinking of cats. You move as silently and dangerously as they do.'

The white-faced, dark-haired young man bowed imperceptibly.

'I am Your Grace's most faithful servant.'

'So you are, Theobald Foliot.'

She studied Foliot's long, narrow face, the eyes that never seemed to blink, bloodless lips above a square jaw, his hair cropped close to his head. He was dressed in a velvet jerkin of blue murrey with matching hose. The belt slung round his narrow waist carried dagger and sword. She watched him beat one leather glove against his hand. When he went to kneel, Elizabeth smiled and patted the seat beside her.

'Sit down, Theobald.'

'Your Grace is most kind.'

'Your Grace could be even kinder.' Elizabeth glanced sideways at him. 'You, Theobald, are my principal clerk.' She leaned towards him. 'Tell me, now, Theobald, when was the last time you went on pilgrimage to Canterbury?'

In his opulent chamber that overlooked Saint Ragadon's Hospice, Peter Talbot sat on the edge of his canopied bed, listening to the sounds from the street below. Small, thickset, with balding head and florid face, Talbot had a reputation as a shrewd and ruthless wool merchant with fingers in more pies than even the parish gossips knew. He had built up a trade which spanned the Narrow Seas, investing in banking, as well as procuring loans to the new king at Westminster. He should have been riding high but, on that morning of the Feast of Saint Florian, Peter Talbot was worried. He rubbed his face in his hands and stared down at the tip of his polished leather boots specially imported from Cordova. The words of the gospel ran through his mind. 'What does it profit a man if he gain the whole world yet lose his immortal soul?' Am I losing my soul, Talbot wondered? Why did he have this feeling of unease, a premonition of danger, of dark terrors lurking in the shadows? He was a leading burgess of the city; a man personally known to the King. However, since that incident with the witch, Talbot's life had changed, and over something so simple! The merchant owned cottages in the parish of Hackington across the River Stour, a useful source of ready cash. One of his tenants had defaulted and Talbot's young wife, impetuous as ever and with a quick eye to a profit, had turned the tenant out and leased the cottage to another.

'She shouldn't have done that,' Talbot muttered to himself. 'Isabella should have consulted with me!'

The first he knew about it had been the previous Sunday when they had attended Mass in Saint Alphage's church. Talbot had been standing in the porch when a grimy-faced old woman, her stick tapping the flagstones, had crawled like a spider into the church. She'd stopped before him, hand outstretched.

'Cursed be you!' she shrieked. 'Fat lord of the soil though you fly as high as the eagle you shall be brought as low as hell!'

Talbot had just stared in stupefaction, but then his brother Robert had told him that the old woman was Mathilda Sempler, a self-confessed witch and the former tenant of one of his cottages. Robert had laughed and slapped him on the shoulder.

'Don't worry,' he brayed in his trumpet-like voice. 'You are not frightened of some silly, old bitch, an evil-smelling crone!'

Isabella, her fair face flushed, eyes hot with anger, lips curled with disdain, had stood behind Robert nodding in agreement.

'You can't put her back!' Isabella had almost spat the words out. 'She wasn't paying her rent. The cottage has been leased to another.' She'd tossed her head and glared furiously at her husband. 'Surely you won't contradict me?'

Talbot had reluctantly agreed. The old crone had slithered away. He had forgotten about the incident until the curse, written in blood on the skin of an ass, had been found pinned to his front door. Talbot felt in his wallet and drew the skin out.

'*May you be consumed as coal upon the hearth.*' Talbot quietly mouthed the words.

May you shrink as dung upon the wall.
May you dry up as water in a pail.
May you become as small, much smaller than the hip
    bone of a flea.
May you fall
As low as me.

'I didn't know the old bitch could write,' Talbot muttered.

He pushed the curse back into his wallet and sprang to his feet as his wife strode into the room. Talbot took one look at her pretty, shrewish face and groaned. This had been a May and December marriage. Isabella had appeared so coy yet so delightful in bed. Now she was shrewish, intent on amassing influence and power within this merchant's house. She turned, hand on hip. Talbot admired her slender waist, the swell of the generous breasts under her tight-fitting, blue samite dress.

'Husband, you should go down to the stalls.'

She went over to the window and stared down where the apprentices were busily putting out the goods ready for another day's trading. Suddenly she started.

'There's someone stealing! Good Lord, two or three of them! Peter, quickly, come!'

Isabella rushed out of the room. Talbot grabbed his cloak and followed. Isabella was now at the foot of the long and steep stairs, beckoning him to come. Talbot went after her but then he tripped: for a few seconds his whole body rose in the air. He saw the steep fall below him and momentarily recalled Sempler's twisted face and hissed curses. Then Peter Talbot fell through the air, his body spinning and turning, his head and neck striking the balustrade along the stairs until he crashed to the paving stones, head askew, neck completely broken.

Chapter 1

Kathryn Swinbrooke, physician, leech and apothecary in the King's city of Canterbury, had started the day so well. She'd been up just after dawn. She'd scrubbed her body with a sponge soaked in soap from Castille and quickly dressed, pulling down over her petticoats a brown, workday, fustian dress. She now carefully arranged a white wimple around her head to hide the few greying hairs on the side of her temple, then carefully studied her face in the polished piece of steel which served as a mirror.

'The eyes and face, Kathryn, tell you a lot about the body: its humours, the state of mind. Perhaps even a glimpse into the soul.'

Kathryn recalled her dead father's kindly ways. A physician of repute, he was forever quoting all the medical axioms and aphorisms he had learnt. She stared into the mirror. Colum had called her complexion creamy.

'More like chalk,' Kathryn groaned to herself. But, there again, she always went pale after her monthly courses. Am I pretty, she wondered, feeling strangely guilty at this prick of vanity. Her eyes were large and dark, the eyebrows black and finely etched. Her nose was straight but turned up a little at the end; her father always used to tease her about this. He would tap her cheek.

'Sure signs of stubbornness,' he'd remark. 'Generous lips and a firm chin.'

Kathryn glimpsed the few grey hairs. 'You'll pass scrutiny.' She sighed. 'Today I must do the accounts.'

'You must also stop talking to yourself!'

Kathryn started. Thomasina her nurse, helpmate, confidante, counsellor and tyrant of a housekeeper stood in the door of the bed chamber. Kathryn studied her nurse's plump, cheery face, brown button eyes and the way she wore her wimple, more like a war banner than a head-dress.

'You look set for battle, Thomasina.'

Thomasina stared down at her hands and wrists, still covered with traces of flour.

'Some people work and some people sit.' Thomasina chirped, her fleshy cheeks quivering in indignation. She pointed to the window where the sun was streaming through the shutters. 'Spring has truly come, Mistress. I have been out in the garden. The gelda roses are beginning to bud. Even the dog mercury,' Thomasina preened herself on her knowledge of herbs, 'is beginning to show life.' She walked over and looked at Kathryn. 'Which is more than I can say for some people round here!' Breathing heavily, she sat down and took Kathryn's hand in hers. 'Your courses are finished?'

Kathryn smiled and rubbed her stomach. Thomasina leaned over and kissed her softly on the cheek.

'Mine have long gone,' she whispered. 'I am an old tree with no sap.'

'Nonsense!' Kathryn squeezed Thomasina's podgy fingers. 'You will marry again, Thomasina. Mark my words!'

'I have been married three times,' Thomasina replied, blinking back her tears. She stared down at the rush-covered floor. 'I just wish one of my children had survived, little Thomas or Richard. Sometimes,' she glanced at Kathryn, and the tears welled over and ran down her cheeks, 'Sometimes, on a morning like this, out in the garden, with the cuckoo warbling high in the trees and the birds chattering like monks in a choir stall, I feel they are with me dancing about, but I blink and stare, it's only the sunbeams.' Thomasina breathed in noisily through her nose. 'There, I have had my little moan.' She wiped her eyes quickly with her fingers. 'I look forward to your children.'

'I am not married, Thomasina. Well,' Kathryn caught her lip between her teeth. 'Well, you do know what I mean?'

'Aye.' Thomasina put her arm around Kathryn's shoulders. You are married all right, Thomasina reflected, to that cruel-hearted, bare-faced bastard, Alexander Wyville who beat and ill-treated you before swaggering off to join the rebels.

'How long is it?' Kathryn asked, as if she could read Thomasina's thoughts.

'Long enough.'

Kathryn sat up. Thomasina marked how drawn her face had become.

'Do you think he's dead?'

'He's been gone over a year, child,' Thomasina replied. 'He changed his name, but he's gone to his own reward.' She pinched Kathryn's cheek playfully. 'Forget him. If he has not returned within two years and a day I am sure that, if you apply to the arch-deacon's court, you will be given permission to marry again.'

'But Thomasina,' Kathryn declared coyly, 'Whom on earth could I choose?'

'Well, there's Roger Chaddedon,' Thomasina said tartly, refer-ring to the handsome widower and wealthy physician, who lived in Queningate. She caught Kathryn's frown. 'Of course,' Thomasina cooed, 'There's always our Irishman.'

Kathryn grinned.

'He dotes on you.'

'He also dotes on his horses!' Kathryn snapped.

'He is handsome,' Thomasina teased. 'Tall, with strong legs. Men with strong legs are very good in . . .'

'That's enough!' Kathryn snapped, rising to her feet. 'As you say, spring is here. There are tasks to be done.'

Kathryn went downstairs and broke her fast on rabbit stew mixed with onions, small loaves smeared with butter and a jug of watered ale. Shortly afterwards her first patient arrived, Wartlebury, the miller's apprentice, complaining of a wart on his face. Kathryn gave him an infusion of purple spurge. She also advised that if the love of his life would not take him, warts and all, then she didn't really deserve his attention. Wartlebury fairly skipped from the house. Edith and Eadwig, the tanner's twins, came next. They looked like peas out of the same pod. They always talked together and moaned loudly about pains in their stomach and the looseness of their stools.

'In other words, you have diarrhoea,' Kathryn remarked bluntly. She gave them a small jug of heatherlene. 'Drink water,' she advised. 'Nothing but water for the next twenty-four hours. Mix some honey with two horn spoons of this: allow it to mingle in the water.'

'How long?' Edith and Eadwig chorused.

'About the space of ten Aves,' Kathryn replied. 'Drink it four or five times a day. By tomorrow afternoon you will feel much better.'

'But we can't eat!' the twins wailed.

Kathryn crouched down and put a hand on each of their shoulders.

'No, you must let the evil humour go. Promise me. Come back tomorrow and, if you are better, Thomasina will give you some marchpane freshly baked and covered in sugar. Oh, and by the way.' Kathryn stood up and touched both children on the nose. 'You wouldn't have diarrhoea if you hadn't eaten so many fresh berries. I have told you that before.'

Both children stared crestfallen up at her.

'Now, remember, the marchpane tomorrow.'

The two children hurried off. Kathryn went into her chancery to draw up her accounts. Colum had remarked that, perhaps in the summer, the King might levy a new tax. She nibbled at the feathery quill. Her household now was comprised of four: herself, Thomasina, Agnes the maid and Wuf, the foundling boy she had taken into her house the previous summer.

'Waifs and strays,' she murmured.

Both Agnes and Wuf were orphans. Of course, there was also Colum Murtagh, King's Commissioner in Canterbury and keeper of the royal stables out at Kingsmead to the north of the city. Kathryn put her quill down and half listened to Agnes and Thomasina's chattering in the kitchen. They were crushing herbs whilst waiting for the baked bread to cool. They'd placed this in wire baskets and hoisted these up, just under the beams, away from the scavenging mice. In the garden Wuf, already a skilled hand at carpentry, was making a bird box in the hope that some of the sparrows would nest there.

They are not the problem, Kathryn thought.

Colum Murtagh was: the tousle-haired, swarthy-faced Irishman was never absent for long from her thoughts. Handsome in a harsh way with a suntanned face and dark blue eyes, which could twinkle with mischief but become cold and hard as stone. Kathryn shivered, not from fear but uncertainty. No man, not even Alexander Wyville, her errant husband, had touched her soul as deeply as Murtagh. Yet Kathryn was wary. Alexander had been violent where Colum was not, but he had the professional soldier's harsh ruthlessness. She had seen him take a man's head as easily as Thomasina would snip a flower. She listened to the sound of raised voices from the kitchen.

'And, of course, the Irishman will be back to eat,' Thomasina trumpeted in the hope Kathryn would hear. 'He'll be back. Just you wait, as soon as darkness falls, clumping his muddy boots over my freshly scrubbed floor and licking his lips as hungrily as a wolf. It's time,' Thomasina's voice rose almost to a bellow, 'that he stayed out at Kingsmead!'

Kathryn grinned. When Murtagh first arrived, the royal manor at Kingsmead had been derelict so he had taken lodgings with her. The parishioners at Saint Mildred's had gossiped, particularly her kinsman Joscelyn and his viper-tongued wife, but Kathryn didn't care. Colum was an honourable man. She had been reluctant to allow him to stay, but now she was fearful of him leaving. Kathryn breathed in slowly, put down her quill and walked along to the passageway to the shop, which she planned to open after Eastertide. The shelves, which Colum and Wuf had put up, gleamed under their coat of polish. New cupboards stood just within the door and the huge counter had been scrubbed, smoothed down and restained. Sconces for cresset torches had been rivetted to the walls whilst the window, which looked out over the street, had been cleaned and the cracked panes replaced with oiled paper.

Kathryn took the bunch of keys that hung on a cord from her belt and undid the lock to the small store-room at the side of the shop. She closed her eyes and relished the sweetness of nipplewort, goats beard, tarragon, thyme and basil. She had grown some of these herself. Other herbs, like black poplar and white clover, she had bought from tradesmen either in London or Canterbury. She looked down at the strongbox where the phials and small jars of poison were safely locked away: the mushrooms, 'devils bolatus', 'Destroying Angel', or, even rarer, the ground leaves and bark of the boxwood plant. Luberon, the chubby, garrulous city clerk, had promised her that now the city council had been reconstituted, she would, within the month, receive her licence to trade. Kathryn was determined, once it was issued, to begin immediately. She looked around, pronounced herself satisfied and was about to walk back to her chancery when there was a knock on the door and a dirty face peered through.

'Mistress, you have got to come now!' The urchin jumped up and down.

'Why Catslip?' Kathryn smiled at the little beggar boy who helped out at the Poor Priests Hospital.

'Father Cuthbert, he says if you don't come now, the person will die but, if you do come, he will still die.' The boy paused, hands to his lips in puzzlement. 'It doesn't make sense, does it?'

'No, it doesn't,' Kathryn retorted. 'But I'll come anyway.'

She collected her basket of potions and told Thomasina where she was going. Thomasina immediately seized her own cloak, loudly declaring she'd accompany her.

'Look after the house. Don't let anyone in,' Thomasina ordered Agnes, standing round-eyed at the table. 'I don't care if they are dying. And tell Wuf I have counted every, and I mean every, sugared almond in that dish in the pantry.'

Then she swept down the passageway after Kathryn.

'I'd best come with you,' she gasped, clutching on to her mistress. 'You never know about these hospitals, do you?'

'No, no,' Kathryn tactfully replied. 'You don't.'

She kept her own counsel. Long before Kathryn was born, Thomasina had been fond of, even deeply in love with, the ascetic, gentle-eyed Father Cuthbert, the supervisor of Saint Mary's hospital for poor priests. They turned the corner and left Ottemelle Lane, going across to Hetherman Lane whilst Catslip skipped in front of them shouting, 'You'd better hurry! He's going to die! He's going to die!'

Father Cuthbert was waiting in the entrance to the hospital. He grasped Kathryn's hand and peered shortsightedly at her.

'So good of you to come. I am sorry to trouble you but . . .'

'There's no problem.' Thomasina bustled forward and grasped the old priest's hand.

Father Cuthbert blushed with embarrassment.

'We'd best go upstairs.'

He led them up into a long, well-lit chamber, smelling of soap, polish and crushed herbs. Three candle wheels hung from a great black beam, which spanned the length of a room that was divided by curtains hanging from brass rails. Each of these contained a pallet bed, stool and a small table. Most of the incumbents were elderly priests, sent there by the archdiocese so that they could die in some degree of comfort and dignity. Servitors dressed in brown robes padded quietly about with trays or jars. Most of these were poor priests, unable to obtain a benefice, who lived in the hospital and served the sick. Kathryn caught Father Cuthbert by the sleeve of his dusty black gown.

'Father, is it a priest who is dying?'

'Oh no.' Father Cuthbert stopped so suddenly, Thomasina almost collided with him. He rubbed the tip of his sharp nose, his eyes wide in surprise. 'No, it's not a priest, Mistress! But a Frenchman, he's walked all the way from Dover. Come, see for yourself.'

They reached the end of the room. Cuthbert pulled aside the dividing curtain. Kathryn took one look at the man lying against the crisp, white bolster, the blanket sheet tucked up to his chin, and recognised he was dying. A grey, cadaverous face, long and drawn under an untidy mop of white hair. The man kept fingering the blankets. Every so often he would cough and a trickle of blood-tinged spittle drooled from the corner of his mouth.

Kathryn sat on a stool next to the bed and felt the man's skin. It was hot and dry. He started forward, coughing and spluttering, a terrible sound wrenched from his chest. The man lay back on the pillow, his yellow-stained tongue licking dry lips. Kathryn stared helplessly at Father Cuthbert.

'He is feverish?'

'Sometimes,' the priest replied. 'Kathryn, can you help?'

The physician pulled back the bed sheets. The patient was dressed in a simple linen nightshirt buttoned to the neck. She undid this and pressed her ear against his chest, as her father had trained her, to detect the evil humours filling his lungs. She listened carefully as the man gasped for breath, fighting against the constricting rottenness in his lungs.

'I cannot do much.' Kathryn sat up. 'Father, this man needs a priest rather than a physician.' She studied the saliva frothing between the man's lips, the blood had turned a dark red. 'He will die. Probably within the day. All I can do is make him comfortable.'

She asked Thomasina to pass the basket. Father Cuthbert brought a small pewter cup; Kathryn prepared an infusion of sage mixed with water and balm and forced it between the man's lips. The patient, lying listlessly, opened his mouth as Kathryn poured this down his throat. Kathryn laid his head back on the pillow. She was preparing an opiate to help him sleep when the man's eyes suddenly opened. Kathryn was surprised at the vivacity and intelligence of his look.

'I can speak English,' he whispered.

'What is your name?' Kathryn said.

'I have many names. I was baptised Matthias. In my foolishness I took the name of the demon, Azrael.'

Father Cuthbert gasped, and the patient turned to stare full at the priest.

'God forgive me, Father. In my time I was a sorcerer, a dabbler in the black arts. You must shrive me of my sins: they are as many and as red as gleaming coals.' The man stared round the room as if an invisible presence thronged about his bed. 'The demons gather,' he croaked. 'They have come for my soul. Ah, Jesus Miserere!'

Father Cuthbert grasped the man's hand.

'No soul can be lost,' the priest said, 'who wishes to be saved. But what are you doing in Canterbury?'

'I came on pilgrimage to Saint Thomas' tomb. No, no,' the man rasped. He paused, turning his head sideways, as his whole body was convulsed by a wracking cough. 'Many years ago in Paris I was a master necromancer. I owned a grimoire and used it

18

for great evil, but lost it to another magician, a man with a black heart and no soul, called Tenebrae.' He paused to wet his lips. 'I came to take it back and burn it.'

Father Cuthbert's old, tired face became a mask of fear and concern.

'Tenebrae,' the dying man insisted. 'You have heard of him?'

'I warn my patients against him,' Kathryn replied slowly. 'He is a man of, reputedly, great powers. No one dares move against him.'

The patient grasped her hand.

'Because he has secrets,' he said. 'Tenebrae harrows the human soul. He gleans what he wants, then uses it for blackmail or protection.'

He began to cough so wrackingly Kathryn and Father Cuthbert had to help him up against the bolsters. The spasm left the man exhausted. He rested, then lifted his head.

'I came to Canterbury,' he gasped. 'But I felt so ill, a good woman brought me here.' He smiled thinly. 'May God bless her! I did not see Tenebrae or demand the return of my book.'

'What book?' Kathryn asked.

'The Book of Shadows. The grimoire of Honorius: it contains secret incantations and magic spells. The pathway for demons to enter our world.' His face became more flushed, his eyes glittering with an inner frenzy. 'It must be destroyed!'

'Hush!' Kathryn stroked his face and turned towards Thomasina, who handed over the opiate. Kathryn raised this to the man's lips. He shook his head.

'No! No!' he pleaded with Father Cuthbert. 'In a little while I will drink it. First, you must shrive me, Father. Put the sacrament on my tongue and anoint me with the holy oils.' He forced a weak smile. 'Then, Mistress, I will drink your potion.'

Kathryn had no choice but to agree. She handed the small cup to Father Cuthbert. Thomasina packed up the basket of medicines and herbs. They all left the cubicle and walked down the hospital room to the top of the stairs. Father Cuthbert's gentle face was now surprisingly hard.

'I now remember Tenebrae,' he remarked. 'A sinister magus. I must write to the Archbishop's court. It is a scandal that such evil is tolerated.'

'But why?' Thomasina asked, eager to bring herself to the old man's attention.

'He has patients,' the priest replied. 'Both at court and in this city and, God forgive them, even in the church itself.'

Father Cuthbert grasped Kathryn by the arm.

'But you have done what you can, Mistress Swinbrooke. I thank you. I must hear the man's confession.'

Kathryn made her farewells and went down the stairs. Thomasina lingered. She caught the priest by his warm, soft hands. Cuthbert looked at her, his eyes child-like in their innocence.

'Thomasina, what is the matter?'

'You are well?'

'As fine as can be expected, God be thanked!'

'Well,' Thomasina stuttered, 'I'd best be gone.' She turned and walked down the stairs.

'Thomasina!'

The old nurse turned and stared up at Father Cuthbert.

'I, too, think of you every day.'

Thomasina smiled, then continued more slowly down the stairs, brushing at the tears pricking her eyes. She joined Kathryn outside in the street. Lost in their own thoughts, they walked back down Hethenman Lane until Kathryn decided she wished to buy some sweetmeats for Wuf, so they went up towards Jewry.

'The lad deserves it,' Kathryn declared, hoping her chatter would soothe the distress Thomasina felt whenever she met Father Cuthbert. 'Wuf has been a good boy and . . .' She stopped as they turned the corner of Jewry where a huge crowd had gathered. Kathryn glimpsed the tabards and livery of the city bailiffs.

They had an old woman, cords wrapped round her arms, her hands securely tied; they were shouting at the crowd, waving their staffs to make way. However, the crowd was turning ugly. Stones and clods of mud were thrown and the old woman, her dirty, grey hair hanging over her face, cowered against the wall of a house. 'She's a bloody murderess and a witch!' someone shouted. 'She should hang now!'

'Burn the bitch!'

'Who is it?' Kathryn asked a bystander.

The woman leaned closer and grinned maliciously in a display of rotting teeth, her breath so rank, Kathryn found it hard not to flinch.

'Why it's Mistress Sempler. Haven't you heard the news? She cursed Peter Talbot, sent him flying through the air she did, till he broke his neck at the foot of the stairs.'

Kathryn sighed. She and Thomasina knew Mistress Sempler as a loudmouthed, smelly and rather dirty old woman who lived by herself. Yet, beneath the roughness, she had a heart of gold and had often instructed Kathryn in her secret lore of herbs and potions.

'God help the poor woman,' Thomasina whispered.

Kathryn wondered whether to intervene. She wished Colum or the city clerk Luberon was with her. However, three more bailiffs led by their burly captain whom Kathryn faintly recognised, strode up the street, swords drawn. Their arrival was greeted by more catcalls, but the sight of naked steel and the determined expression on the captain's face forced the crowd to disperse. Kathryn approached one of the escort.

'Is it true?' she asked.

The fellow turned, his face podgy and water coloured. He had a fresh cut just beneath his eye and glared in pig-eyed fury at the physician.

'Piss off and mind your own business!'

Thomasina pushed her way between them. 'That's no way to

talk to a lady, fathead!' She thrust her face only a few inches from his. 'This, my dear maggot, is Kathryn Swinbrooke, physician of the city, friend of Master Luberon as well as Colum Murtagh the King's Commissioner.'

The bailiff paled and stepped away as the captain intervened. He doffed his hat of squirrel fur and fairly danced from foot to foot as he tried to adopt a more tactful approach.

'My apologies, Mistress,' he gabbled. 'But the news is all over the city.'

Kathryn looked round at the cowering, old woman.

'So, Peter Talbot is dead?'

'Aye, as cold as carrion meat. He fell downstairs this morning. His wife and kinsfolk think it's magic.' He nodded at Sempler. 'She has confessed to casting a spell and placing it under his door.'

'May I speak to her?'

The captain agreed and stood aside.

Kathryn approached Mathilda, crinkling her nose at the sour smell from the old woman's dirt-stained gown.

'Mathilda.' She put her hands on the old crone's shoulder. 'Mathilda, it's me, Kathryn Swinbrooke.'

The old woman parted the veil of her greasy grey hair: one eye was bloodshot and her lower lip was beginning to swell.

'Oh, don't hurt me,' Sempler whimpered.

'Did you do it?' Kathryn asked.

'I cast a spell,' the woman whined, failing to recognise Kathryn. 'But he thrust me out of my cottage. He left me like a dog to wander the alley-ways.'

Kathryn squeezed the woman's bony shoulder. 'I'll see what I can do.'

She stepped back and the bailiffs gathered round. One of them gave a tug at the rope and Mathilda was dragged further up the street. The captain came back.

'Mistress, there's nothing we can do. The Talbots are powerful.

She has confessed her guilt.' He lowered his voice. 'She'll burn. The King's Justices of Assize are due in the city. She'll find no mercy with them.' And, spinning on his heel, he walked away.

Kathryn forgot about the marchpane or the sweet comfits for Wuf and walked back towards Ottemelle Lane. Thomasina tried to draw her into conversation but Kathryn felt a deep despair. Mathilda Sempler was a crazy old woman, but would she be burnt to death because of a silly curse? Kathryn recalled the patient at the Poor Priests Hospital and the spring day lost some of its freshness. Her father had always warned her about this. How, when the winter died and the roads and lanes were opened, the juices began to run through nature and people gave free rein to the strange phantasms which lurked in their souls: sorcery, magic and the fear of hell's legions. Canterbury seemed to attract such bizarre mummery. Kathryn glimpsed a huge mastiff being led by its wealthy owner up a street. The dog was securely muzzled and on its back rode a dwarf, a yellow bell cap upon his head and a white wand in his hand. Between the stalls, outside a row of houses, a man shouted that he could chew burning charcoal in his mouth. Further down an old woman declaimed how she could drink a gallon of beer yet vomit more than she had drunk. Strangely dressed chanters offered to recite poems or tell stories about mythical lands in the East. At the mouth of an alley-way, two blind men, strapped back to back, did a strange dance over burning brands, the hungry flames narrowly missing their skin, much to the delight of the small crowd that had gathered to watch them burn. She recalled Colum's words.

'On earth,' the Irishman had remarked, 'angels walk and so do demons. Unfortunately it's the demons who make their presence felt.'

They turned into Ottemelle Lane and almost bumped into Colum and Luberon.

'We were coming to look for you.' The Irishman gripped Kathryn by the arm and smiled down at her, then his face became grave.

'Why?' Kathryn asked.

'The magician, Tenebrae,' Luberon declared. 'He's been foully murdered!'

Chapter 2

K athryn took Colum and Luberon back to the house. Whilst Thomasina prepared some beef and mushroom stew and sliced the freshly baked bread, Colum explained his abrupt return from Kingsmead.

'Master Luberon arrived.' He gestured at his companion. 'And told me Tenebrae was dead.'

'How?' Kathryn asked.

'A crossbow bolt, embedded firmly in his throat.'

'Only this morning,' Kathryn offered, 'I visited a patient at the Poor Priests Hospital who was travelling to see Tenebrae.' She then explained briefly her visit to Father Cuthbert and Luberon's face grew graver. 'What is so important about this man?'

Luberon sipped the wine and smiled shyly at Thomasina, who blushed and simpered back.

'When you are ready?' Kathryn teased.

Luberon put the cup down. 'In our lives, Kathryn,' he said, 'everything is simple. I am Simon Luberon, clerk to His Grace the Archbishop of Canterbury. I have my own little house, my daily routine, my friends.' He glanced archly at Thomasina. 'And those whom I always think about. I attend Mass on Sundays, sometimes, even during the working week. I pay my tithes and taxes. I do my best to follow the law of God and uphold the rule of the King's writ.' He paused, breathing in noisily through his fleshy nostrils, his merry eyes now sombre. 'That is the world I live in, as do you. But Tenebrae was a magus. His world was thronged by spells, curses, incantations, waxen effigies, blood sacrifices and blasphemous rituals.'

'So, why didn't the Church arrest him?' Kathryn interrupted, slightly impatient at Luberon's lugubrious tone.

'Ah, Tenebrae is no village warlock dealing in petty spells,' Luberon replied. 'He really did believe in, and practise, the black arts. His customers were wealthy. More important, Tenebrae was a professional blackmailer. He acquired knowledge about the mighty of this land, which should best be left secret. That's why I went out to Kingsmead to bring back Colum Murtagh, the King's Commissioner. Believe me, as soon as Tenebrae's death is known in London, the King will make his power felt.'

'I can't see why,' Kathryn said. 'Surely the Church will be full of people thanking God he is dead.' She glanced across at Colum who sat, chin in hand, listening intently to the conversation.

Luberon brushed the crumbs from his velvet jerkin, his fleshy jowls quivering in righteous anger.

'Of course, Tenebrae's death won't worry them but he had a book, a folio of spells, the grimoire of Honorius.'

'The Book of Shadows,' Kathryn breathed. 'That's how the man dying in the Poor Priests Hospital described it.'

Luberon nodded. 'Yes, the Book of Shadows. It not only contained spells and magical formulae, Tenebrae also listed his secrets there: that book is now missing. Whether you like it or not, Kathryn, Colum will be ordered to investigate the death and recover the book whilst you, as city physician hired specially by the Royal Council, will also have a role to play.'

'Not necessarily,' Colum intervened. 'There's no need for

Kathryn's involvement in this business: it's murder straight and simple.'

Luberon coughed and glanced sideways at the dark-faced Irishman. The clerk was always wary of Colum. Oh, he liked Murtagh with his unruly shock of hair, swarthy features and dry sense of humour. However, like Kathryn, Luberon sensed his ruthlessness, whilst he was only a man of the chancery, skilled in the use of parchment and quill not the sword, dagger and mace.

'Oh, wisest of clerks,' Colum murmured, 'if I hold my breath any longer I'll expire.'

Luberon rubbed his chin. 'First, Master Murtagh, no offence, but Kathryn's sharp eye and skilful scrutiny is now well known to the court. Second, Kathryn holds an indenture with the city council. As you may remember, that council was dissolved because of Canterbury's adherence to the House of Lancaster. Its rights and privileges have now been renewed. The city council wants to please the King in this matter. They will insist on Kathryn's involvement. And, finally,' Luberon paused, scratching his cheek nervously.

'Oh, come, Simon!' Colum snapped, winking at Kathryn.

'Mistress Swinbrooke,' the clerk hastily added, 'knows a great deal about potions.' He smiled apologetically. 'Don't take offence, but the line between medicine and magic is very thin.'

'The devil,' Kathryn interrupted sharply, 'is not a physician.'

'True, true,' Luberon replied. 'You may also have a personal interest in the matter. Your husband Alexander Wyville? There's not much Tenebrae didn't know. I wonder if this grimoire held information about him?'

Kathryn glanced away: Thomasina stood at the hearth, her back turned to them, though listening intently to every word. Agnes was outside, hanging sheets to dry in the warm, spring sun; Wuf had given up his carpentry and was now hunting snails.

Will the past ever go away? Kathryn thought. Alexander Wyville, why don't you die and let me have peace?

'Mistress Swinbrooke!'

Kathryn glanced back at Luberon.

'It would be best if we began now. We must hasten to Tenebrae's house. The Council would like to declare they have matters in hand.'

Kathryn reluctantly agreed. Colum finished his wine, shouting across to Thomasina that they would eat the stew on their return.

'I work my fingers to the bone for you, Irishman,' Thomasina wailed, 'and what do I get?'

'Bony fingers, I suppose, Mistress Thomasina.' Colum stepped aside as the nurse threw a cloth at his head.

'What passion.' Colum laughed. 'Master Luberon, have you ever seen so much passion in one woman?'

The little clerk blushed with embarrassment and shuffled to his feet. Kathryn came back from her chancery office, cloak over one arm; she carried a leather pannier, which contained her writing instruments. Colum took this from her and slung it over his shoulder. He was about to continue his teasing of Thomasina when Luberon plucked him by the sleeve.

'Irishman, a word?'

As Kathryn went over to talk to Thomasina, Colum followed Luberon out down the passage to the front door.

'What is it, man?' Colum said testily.

Luberon looked back towards the kitchen and waited for Kathryn to join them.

'This business,' the clerk explained. 'It won't be the King who wants Tenebrae's death investigated. According to the gossip, the dead magus was patronised by the queen, Elizabeth Woodville.'

Colum's stomach lurched. He felt a chill as if a sudden rush of cold air had swept through the house.

'What does that mean?' Kathryn asked.

'Edward the King,' Colum replied, 'is as magnanimous as he is big. He loses his temper on Monday and forgets it on Tuesday, but the Queen is different. She's a very dangerous woman. No injury, no slight, no threat is ever forgotten.' Colum sighed. 'She'll want her way in this business. If I fail her, she'll never forget.'

He threw open the door and went out into the street, not even bothering to answer Thomasina's farewells.

Kathryn and Luberon hurried behind him. They went up Hethenman Lane, turning left at the top into King Street, the broad thoroughfare, which ran towards Holy Cross Church near the western gate of the city. Kathryn would have liked to have questioned Luberon further but this proved impossible. It was now early afternoon and the market stalls were doing a roaring trade as throngs of pilgrims made their way through to worship before Becket's tomb. Apprentices screamed at the tops of their voices, offering ribbons, cloths from Ghent, needles from London, leather goods and bottles from Bristol.

'What do you lack?' they cried. 'What do you lack?'

The cookshops and taverns were also busy: the air was thick with the fresh meat being cooked or grilled in tangy, spicy sauces. Beggars whined at every corner. Two men, with black holes where their eyes had been, wandered about hand in hand: they claimed they had been cruelly treated by Turks on pilgrimage to Jerusalem and now threw themselves on the mercy of good Christian folk. A relic-seller, his trays laid out on the steps of a church, roared that he had the most holy artefacts blessed by the Pope himself and attested by the College of Cardinals: a napkin used by the Lord Jesus at the Last Supper; a stool fashioned by Saint Joseph; the remains of one of the baskets after Christ had fed the five thousand; a hair of Elijah's beard; the sling of David and, much to Kathryn's astonishment, an ear from the head of Goliath. She watched people stare open-mouthed at this cunning man's tricks and realised how easy it was for the likes of Tenebrae to make a fortune out of foolish superstition, whilst an old woman like Mathilda Sempler could die for it.

In Saint Peter's Street the bailiffs had already rounded up those who had trespassed too far on the credulity of citizens and pilgrims. A tavern master was being forced to stand in a tub full of horse piss, as the placard round his neck attested, a warning to those who mixed water with their ale. Next to him, in the head stocks, a butcher watched mournfully, moving his imprisoned head painfully as market beadles burnt sausages under his nose whilst a crier proclaimed how one Guido Armerger had used cats' meat in his sausages. Petty pilferers, drunken apprentices and a whore, her head shaven so it was bald as a pigeon's egg, were locked in the stocks: all around them, ragged-arsed urchins pelted them with rubbish and dirt plucked from the sewer which ran down the centre of the street. Kathryn glanced away, even putting one hand over her ears, as they passed the city executioner: he was busily branding a blasphemer, pressing his heated iron to the screaming man's face to leave a *B,* a warning that would last for the rest of his life.

As they passed Blackfriars the crowd thinned. Between the overhanging houses on either side, which were festooned with their gaudily painted signs, the road was busy with pedlars and their pack ponies, peasants in their two-wheeled carts now leaving the city after a morning's trading. Kathryn glanced at Luberon: he was beginning to feel the heat, drops of sweat pricked his fleshy face. Kathryn had to shout at Colum to slow down. The Irishman stopped and glanced back at her.

'I am sorry,' he said. 'To be sure, I was far away.' He pulled Kathryn and Luberon out into the shadowy recess of a door. 'Do you want to rest?'

'It's not much further,' Luberon gasped. 'But need you hurry so?'

Colum grinned sheepishly. 'I'll tell you a secret. I have been a soldier and fought in bloody battles but black magic, the laws of the gibbet, the secret rites of the cemeteries, have always frightened me.' He glanced across the street. 'In Ireland, such magic plagues our lives. I want to get this matter over.'

Kathryn wetted her finger and touched Colum on the tip of his nose.

'Come, my little bog trotter, there's more murder than magic here. But, for pity's sake, walk slower or either you, or I, will have to carry Luberon!'

They continued up the street, keeping well away from the sewer, which had now overflowed, and the pigs rooting amongst the rotting refuse. Once they had passed the Friars of the Sack, they turned into Black Griffin Lane. A one-eyed journeyman who sold needles, ribbons and gee-gaws from his tray, with a chattering monkey sitting on his shoulder, told them the way. Kathryn, trying not to look at the dung that encrusted the shoulders of the man's shabby jerkin, followed his simple directions.

'Go round that corner,' the man said throatily. 'You can't miss the sorcerer's house: tall and black as night!'

Colum pulled a face as Kathryn led them on. They turned the corner and, across the street, was Tenebrae's house. The journeyman's description was correct: tall, at least three storeys high, it stood in its own grounds, a narrow alley-way on either side. Kathryn had not been down the lane for years, and she was surprised, as well as slightly fearful, at the house's appearance: black polished beams and gables, even the plaster had been daubed black as night, as were the sills and shutters. The windows were long and spacious, but the thick glass had been tinted a dull grey to prevent anyone peering in. Above the broad doorway was a shield with a red-gold mandrake root gilded upon it. Two bailiffs wearing city livery stood, swords drawn, at the wicket gate, politely refusing entry to a group of richly dressed burgesses.

Colum pushed his way through. The bailiffs recognised both him and Luberon and ordered the group to stand aside.

'Why should we?' their leader exclaimed. A tall, fleshy-faced man with grey streaks of hair, he was dressed in a velvet, fur-edged, woollen robe: his fat fingers, covered with glittering rings, played with the gold guild chain round his neck.

'Because I am Colum Murtagh, King's Commissioner in Canterbury!' the Irishman declared softly. 'This is Master Simon Luberon, clerk of the city council; the lady is Mistress Kathryn Swinbrooke, physician. And who, sir, are you?'

The man drew himself up, puffing his chest out like a peacock as if to display his expensive sarcanet doublet.

'I am Sir Raymond Hetherington of Cheapside,' the portly merchant replied. 'Banker and, indeed, friend of His Grace the King.'

Colum looked at the man's hard, little eyes, thick, black eyebrows, nose as sharp as a quill and the petulant cast of his lips. He sketched a bow.

'Sir Raymond, I have heard of you.' Colum glanced round at the rest of the group. 'What business do you have here?'

Hetherington's lips pursed like an old woman's.

'We had business this morning with Master Tenebrae; we are shocked at his death.'

'His murder,' Colum corrected.

Hetherington lost some of his hauteur. 'Yes, yes,' he mumbled. 'His murder.'

He looked over his shoulder at his companions as if seeking their support. Kathryn studied them carefully as Hetherington introduced them. Thomas Greene, goldsmith, thin as a bean pole and sour-faced, with a sallow complexion. Kathryn wondered if he suffered from ill humours of the liver. The widow Dionysia, dressed soberly in dark blue, her face ravaged by age, must have been beautiful in her youth. Beside her a young man Richard Neverett, dressed in a costly cote hardie over a pale cream cambric shirt, woollen green leggings and expensive Spanish leather boots. His fiancée Louise Condosti looked like a fairy princess with her angelic face, wide blue eyes and cluster of blonde hair. Anthony Fronzac, a small, dusty-faced man with tired eyes and a slack mouth, who introduced himself as Clerk to the Guild. Finally, Charles Brissot, London physician: a pleasant-faced, rotund, little man, sparking eyes and red cheeks, a neatly cut moustache and fine, pointed beard. Kathryn hid her smile; her father had always mocked the London physicians with their splendid clothes and glorious apparel. Brissot was certainly one of these. He was garbed in a quilted, orange jerkin with a small, linen ruff at neck and collar, tight hose and elegant shoes whilst, over his shoulders, hung a rather old-fashioned houppelonde, a long cloak of various colours, edged with lamb's-wool. For a while all chattered nervously, slightly awed by this tall, grim-faced Irishman. Kathryn had to pinch Colum gently on the arm because he was already treating them as a group of felons.

'Why can't we go in?' Sir Raymond Hetherington bellowed, eyes bulbous, cheeks blown out like those of a frog.

'Who is inside?' Luberon tactfully asked one of the bailiffs.

'Tenebrae's clerk, Morel,' the fellow replied. 'And a popinjay from court. I didn't quite catch his name, tall and dark.' The fellow turned away and spat. 'He looked dangerous to me.'

Colum ordered Sir Raymond and his party to adjourn to a nearby tavern whilst he and his companions went up the path and hammered on the metal-studded door. Kathryn stared round the garden and shivered.

'It could be quite pleasant,' she observed. 'But look, Colum, nothing but weeds.'

Colum brought the iron knocker, carved in the shape of a devil's face, down once more then followed her gaze.

'Nothing but hemp and flax; even the grass looks tired,' Kathryn whispered. 'Thomasina and I could transform this. We would have herb banks . . .'

Kathryn abruptly paused as she heard the sound of footsteps, then the door swung open. Kathryn almost jumped with fright at the man who stood there: he had a white, podgy, slack face, eyes with no lashes, scrawny brows, balding head and blue, watery eyes. If it hadn't been for the occasional blink, Kathryn would have sworn he was either dead or in some trance. He glared suspiciously at Colum.

'Who are you?' The man's lips hardly moved.

'The King's man,' Murtagh replied, pushing him aside. 'And who are you?'

'Morel, Master Tenebrae's clerk, servant, door keeper, whatever you wish.' Morel moved swiftly to block Colum's way. 'And, if you don't leave, I'll break your neck! The King's man is already here!'

Colum's hand fell to the dagger in his belt.

'Now, now, now!'

The voice was soft. Looking round Morel, Kathryn saw a young man, pale-faced, dressed in a dark purple doublet and hose, come quietly along the corridor. He crossed his arms and leaned against the black-painted wall. Kathryn did not know whether his face was that of an angel or devil; smooth shaven, framed by dark hair, the generous mouth was twisted into a smile, the eyes had that constant look of mockery, as if they only believed a tenth of what they saw. A young face, Kathryn thought, but the eyes were old.

'Now, now!' the man repeated.

He moved languorously, delicately like a woman, yet this made him seem all the more dangerous. He came and stood beside Morel, thumbs pushed in his silver-buckled war belt. Kathryn glimpsed the sword and dagger hanging there as if they were part and parcel of his body.

'So far, you have only said, "Now, now",' Colum remarked. 'Come, sir, do not keep us in suspense.'

The man grinned, put his hand on his heart and bowed mockingly at Kathryn.

'My name is Theobald Foliot, squire and personal equerry of Her Grace, Queen Elizabeth Woodville.' He gestured elegantly at Colum. 'You must be Murtagh the Irishman?' He narrowed his eyes. 'The King trusts you, which is rare for an Irishman.'

34

Before Colum could reply, Foliot took one step forward; he seized Kathryn's hand and, raising it to his cold lips, kissed it expertly.

'And Mistress Kathryn Swinbrooke, renowned physician of the city. Madame, you are most welcome.' He smiled dazzlingly at her. 'The Queen sends you her good wishes. I believe you have met her.'

Kathryn could only blush and stammer with embarrassment, then quickly seized Colum's wrist as he fumed at Foliot's insult. The Queen's emissary caught her movement.

'No, don't do that.' He extended his hand and gave Colum that same smile. 'I was only teasing you, Irishman. No insult was intended.'

'None taken,' Murtagh replied as he grasped the man's hand.

'Well.' Foliot stood back. 'Morel, let us take our guests into the kitchen. Master Luberon,' he said and shook the little clerk's hand, 'let us investigate this dreadful business.'

Morel, who had stood statue-like throughout, shrugged and led them down the dark passageway into a cleanly scrubbed kitchen. Kathryn stared around. After the exterior of the house and the grim hall and passageway, the kitchen was a complete surprise. The floor and tables were scrubbed; gleaming skillets and fleshing knives hung neatly from hooks on the walls. The fire was doused and the oven was cold but the air still smelt fragrantly of spiced meats and freshly baked bread. Foliot made them sit round the great oval oak table whilst, at his command, Morel served them Rhenish wine slightly chilled and a tray of marzipan. He was about to leave but Foliot clicked his fingers and pointed to a stool.

'No, no, Morel, you stay with us. Well?' Foliot leaned his elbows on the table. 'I am the Queen's emissary. I arrived in Canterbury yesterday evening and took lodgings at the White Hart Tavern. Early this morning, just after Matins, I came here to see Master Tenebrae. We had a few words down here in the kitchen as Morel can testify. I then left because of Master Tenebrae's appointments. I believe you met them outside?'

'Sir Raymond Hetherington and his party?' Colum asked.

'The same,' Foliot murmured. 'Apparently every one of them, between the hours of eight and noon today, came for a meeting with our dead friend. Each came at their appointed time.' He smiled down at Morel. 'Then what happened?'

Morel hunched his great shoulders. 'Master had asked for some wine and quince tarts at half-past twelve. I took them up. I knocked on his door but I could hear no answer.'

'And so?' Colum asked.

'I came back downstairs. I thought he might have gone out by the back route. However, a short time later, I went there myself and spoke to Bogbean.'

'Bogbean?' Kathryn interrupted.

'Oh, yes, he's a toper Tenebrae employed to guard the rear entrance of the house. He said the master hadn't left. I became concerned so I went upstairs with a log from the cellar and forced the door.' Morel blinked but, apart from that, his face did not change expression. 'The candles were lit. My master was sitting behind a table. I thought he was asleep. I called out but he didn't move. I went closer . . .'

For the first time Morel showed some emotion, staring down at the table-top, his lips moving soundlessly. Kathryn wondered if he had lost his wits and suffered from some deep sickness of the mind.

'My master was sitting back in his chair,' Morel continued. 'The hood and mask still on his face, the crossbow bolt embedded deep in his throat, only a few splatters of blood.' Morel, as if dream walking, rose to his feet. 'Come, you can see for yourself.'

Colum looked at Foliot who shrugged. They followed the servant along the passageway and up the wooden stairs. The balustrade and newel post were painted black. A writhing devil halfway up greeted them: carved in wood, the demon, in the form of a frog with a man's face, leered at Kathryn and made her shiver.

At the top of the stairs, to the right, was a gallery with two chambers but Morel went ahead into a small recess, pushed open a door and led them into Tenebrae's chamber. Kathryn felt she was entering the darkness of hell. She stared round speechlessly. The room was long and polished. Wooden panelling covered the walls, and the floor-boards had been covered with a black, glossy paint. The candle-holders screwed into the wood were also black as were the candles. She looked up at the painted ceiling and gasped at the awesome, blood-daubed goat surrounded by legions of demons in many forms: some had the heads of monkeys and the bodies of women, others the faces of goats and the limbs of children.

'It's cold,' Kathryn said and then she caught the smell. At first a musty perfume but something else lay beneath it, foul and fetid, like the sour breath from a rotting mouth.

Colum's arm went round her shoulders, he hugged her tightly.

'Lord save us, Kathryn!'

Kathryn stared around. Luberon looked positively ill, his face had become a whitish paste. He stood, wiping the sweat from his palms against his gown. Morel remained as still as a statue whilst Foliot hid his unease by crossing his arms and tapping his feet impatiently against the floor.

Kathryn forced herself to walk forward, towards the table covered in a purple drape; in the shadowy chair behind, she glimpsed Tenebrae's corpse, still squatting in death. Her footsteps sounded hollow, like the beat of a drum. Keeping her eyes on the chair, Kathryn dug her nails deep into the palms of her hand and tried to breathe in deeply through her nose.

It's like a dream, she thought, one of those nightmares when I am flying along a gallery towards some evil lurking in the shadows. Morel gasped, and Kathryn looked down. She was standing in some magic circle: she recognised the triangle and other cabalistic signs and glimpsed further traces of blood. Kathryn stopped.

'In the name of sweet God!' she shouted.

And, to give vent to her feelings and before anyone could stop her, Kathryn walked across the room and pulled back the shutters, throwing the wooden bars to the floor. The window behind was firmly locked but Kathryn undid the clasps and lifted up the latch. She breathed in deeply as air and light flooded into the room.

'You shouldn't do that!' Morel wailed, his podgy hand waving in the air.

Kathryn turned, her face a mask of fury.

'I'll do what I wish!' she shot back. 'This room is sick, it reeks of all that is evil!'

Colum and Luberon joined her and soon the windows on either side of the room were open, the fresh air and sunlight driving away the shadows and menacing atmosphere. Kathryn then strode back to the table and looked down at the artefacts that littered its purple top: a black candle, a collection of dice made out of bone, a quill of raven feathers, an inkpot shaped in the form of a skull, and tarot cards. Kathryn tried not to look at the black-garbed corpse sprawled in the chair but, rolling the table-cloth as if it was a sack, threw it and its disgusting contents to the floor. She glanced up at Foliot and pulled a face.

'I hate this,' Kathryn muttered. 'I detest these lords of the gibbet who prey like rats upon human suspicion and greed.'

She opened her wallet and took out the rosary beads, which had once belonged to her mother and put them round her neck. She glanced quickly at Morel who was now standing like a child, his hands hanging by his side.

'Did you believe all this?'

Morel just stared back.

'If he were so powerful,' Kathryn almost shouted, 'then why did he allow himself to be murdered? If he could see the future, why couldn't he avoid his own death?'

Morel made some strange sign in the air with his podgy fingers.

'Oh, for Heaven's sake!'

Kathryn told Colum to bring one of the candles from their holder and lifted the black mask from the dead man's face.

'Death is a great leveller,' her father had once remarked.

In this case Kathryn had to agree. Tenebrae's face looked no different from many taken unexpectedly by death, the eyes rolled back in their sockets, chin sagging, mouth open. The waxy-coloured cheeks and jowls now were slack. Nothing untoward except for a feeling of unease whenever Kathryn caught the sightless gaze of his eyes, and the large patch of blood, which streamed from the jagged hole in Tenebrae's throat down his chest.

'The blood's congealed,' Kathryn noted. 'What time is it now?'

'About two o'clock,' Luberon replied.

Kathryn touched the man's face. 'Morel, what time did you come up?'

'About half an hour after mid-day when my master rang the bell.'

'And you knocked on the door,' Kathryn insisted.

'Yes, I told you, my master replied: he said he would take his refreshments in a little while.'

'You are sure the room was empty?'

'Of course,' Morel said. 'Bogbean said that the last visitor, Dauncey, had already left.'

Kathryn left the table and walked back towards the door. It was carved out of heavy oak and reinforced with steel bands and metal studs. She studied the smashed lock. Morel followed her like a dog. Kathryn, crouching beside the lock, looked up.

'You smashed this open?'

'Oh, yes!'

'And the door can only be locked and opened from the inside?'

'As I said, my master had the locks on this door, and the one at the far end, specially fashioned by a Cheapside keysmith.'

Kathryn studied the handle, the lock now buckled with the key lying on the floor. She opened the door and studied the other side.

'Your master,' she said, 'must have been a suspicious man. I doubt if even the King's Exchequer in London has doors with handles and locks only on the inside.' She walked back across the room towards the other door, which Luberon already was examining.

'It's the same here!' he cried. 'Look!'

Kathryn passed the table where Colum and Foliot were still examining the corpse. Luberon stood aside and Kathryn found the door, lock and handle were identical to the one at the entrance. She slowly opened the door and, followed by Luberon, went out onto the small landing, which led to the back stairs. Just inside the room, on the left, was a window. Kathryn examined this, but it was firmly shuttered and barred. She opened these, and saw the window clasps and latch were firmly in place. They went down the stairs. The door at the bottom was the same as the ones they had examined upstairs, with handle and lock on the inside. They opened it and stepped into a small alley-way filled with rubbish and reeking of cat urine. Kathryn shook her head and, closing the door, went back up the stairs and into Tenebrae's chamber.

Chapter 3

W'ell,' Colum said, 'Tenebrae's as dead as a piece of mutton.' He lifted the left hand of the corpse and showed her the rings glittering there. 'He still has these on him and a money purse on his belt, so it wasn't robbery.'

'Except for the grimoire of Honorius,' Foliot interrupted.

Kathryn beckoned Morel closer. 'Look.' Kathryn chose her words carefully. 'Look around this room, Master Morel. Apart from the grimoire has anything been stolen or disturbed?'

Morel padded round the room. The chamber had now lost some of its terror. The daylight made it look rather tawdry and pathetic with that great magus sprawled in death, a crossbow bolt buried in his throat. Morel came back, shaking his head solemnly.

'Nothing has been disturbed, Mistress.'

'Then it is a great mystery.' Kathryn sighed. 'This chamber is on the second storey of the house. Along the walls on either side, the windows are firmly latched, the shutters barred, as are the doors at either end and the one downstairs likewise. No one could come into this chamber, or even up the back stairs, without Tenebrae's permission as all doors can only be opened from the inside. Apparently Tenebrae was alive and well when Master Foliot visited him this morning. He then sees his guests whom we have fleetingly met outside. Each one comes up at his or her appointed time. Between what hours, Master Morel?'

'Nine and noon.'

'They all have their meetings,' Kathryn continued, trying to ignore Morel's unwavering gaze. 'They come up the stairs, as we did. Tenebrae lets them out by the far entrance.' She led them to the door at the far end and through into the small gallery. 'They go down and out at the back lest anyone sees them. So who murdered Tenebrae?' She pointed to the window on the landing. 'This is secure, and there are no other entrances, are there?'

Colum said he wasn't certain, so they returned to the death chamber to make a rigorous search, which only confirmed Morel's protests at the futility of their actions. The wainscoting was secure. No trapdoors or secret entrances could be found in the gaudily painted ceiling or black, painted floor.

Kathryn went and studied Tenebrae's corpse.

'Someone,' she said, 'God knows who, came in here with an arbalest and bolt, shot Tenebrae, stole the grimoire and then disappeared.'

'It could have been magic,' Morel spoke up quickly.

'Why magic?' Kathryn asked.

Morel spread his hands. 'My master always said he could be killed by magic.'

Kathryn took a step closer. 'Aren't you sad, Morel? Don't you grieve and mourn for your master?'

The man smiled slyly and pushed his face only a few inches from them. Kathryn stared into his liquid, vacuous eyes; Morel, she realised, was as mad as a March hare.

'My master always said death would not hold him. Another magus will come and free him from the tomb.' Morel breathed in, his nostrils quivering. 'So now I must go. The house must be kept clean. There are tasks to be done.'

And, without further ado, Morel waddled out, closing the door behind him.

'Do you think he murdered his master?' Foliot asked.

Kathryn shook her head. 'I don't know. But treat him gently. Morel has a terrible sickness of the mind or soul, God knows what.' She glanced at Luberon. 'The house should be searched.'

'Oh, I have done that.' Foliot interrupted. 'And what a treasure there is: cups, goblets, plates, ewers, costly drapes, robes.' He shook his head. 'But nothing else.'

Kathryn thought of the jumble and chaos of her own house.

'No accounts?' she exclaimed. 'No indentures, letters?'

'None,' Foliot replied.

'It's the way of such people,' Colum interrupted. 'The grimoire would hold everything. Am I not right, Master Foliot?'

The queen's emissary pulled a face. 'It's why we want that grimoire back.'

'How big is it?' Kathryn asked.

'According to Her Grace,' Foliot said, 'the size of a large church missal, twelve inches high and the same across; she said it is as thick as a door step.'

Kathryn turned and waved round the chamber. 'And who will receive all this?'

'I have already checked the civil records,' Luberon said. 'There is no will or letter of attorney. . . .'

'Accordingly,' Foliot spoke up, 'this house and all its moveables belong to the Crown.' He pointed at Luberon. 'The creature downstairs can stay for a while. However, you, Master Luberon, are the city clerk and you, Murtagh, the King's Commissioner here.' He kicked at the tablecloth Kathryn had thrown on the floor. 'The tools of Tenebrae's trade can be burnt but his possessions are to be placed in a locked chest, sealed and despatched to Westminster. If anyone steals from this house, they steal from the Crown and that's treason.'

'And Tenebrae's death?' Kathryn asked.

Foliot walked slowly towards her, arms still crossed. Kathryn caught the mockery in his eyes.

'Tenebrae's dead,' he said. 'May he rot in hell. There may not be a God in heaven, Mistress Kathryn, but there's certainly a devil in hell. Nor I, nor the Queen, nor His Grace the King give a fig: Tenebrae was a magus and a blackmailer who, at last, received his just deserts. However, as to the grimoire of Honorius, the Book of Shadows, the holder of so many secrets, including the whereabouts of Tenebrae's wealth, I will not leave Canterbury without it. So both of you, in whom Their Graces have so much trust, will find Tenebrae's assassin and the grimoire.' Foliot let his hands drop by his side. 'I am lodged at the White Hart in Queningate, but don't worry, if you don't come looking for me I shall certainly search you out.' And, bowing at Kathryn and nodding at Murtagh, Foliot swaggered from the room.

'Who is he?' Kathryn asked.

'One of Woodville's henchmen,' Colum answered. He paused to choose his words carefully. 'The Queen is a relative commoner, the widow of Sir John Woodville. She caught and now holds the King by her beauty and her skill—some even say by witchcraft. Now, when she rose others followed, men like Foliot, greedy for power. They have one allegiance, one religion, one duty and that is the will of Elizabeth Woodville.'

'And was Tenebrae one of her men?'

'No,' Colum said. 'A creature of the darkness. We don't know Tenebrae's real name or where he came from. When he goes into the ground very few will care. Master Luberon!'

The little clerk waddled over.

'Would you please stay and search around here. Make sure Foliot has told us the truth. Have Tenebrae's corpse removed to the nearest church. Use whatever powers you have to ensure the poor bastard's buried.'

'No priest will sing a Mass over his grave,' Luberon replied dourly.

'A coffin and a blessing: that's all I ask.'

'And you?' Luberon asked.

Colum glanced at Kathryn, who was staring up at the leering goat painted on the ceiling.

'I think we should visit those patrons of Tenebrae. Where's the nearest tavern?'

'The Bishop's Mitre,' Luberon said. 'It's further down Black Griffin Lane.'

'Then we shall join them there. Yes, Kathryn?'

She agreed. They left Luberon and walked down the staircase. Morel was waiting for them at the bottom. He ignored Colum but caught hold of Kathryn's gown.

'Mistress.' His watery eyes pleaded with Kathryn.

'What is it, man?' Colum demanded.

'I was not talking to you!' Morel hissed, his face suddenly becoming ugly.

'What is it, Morel?' Kathryn asked quietly.

'When will he come back?'

Kathryn stared into those mad eyes.

'My master, Tenebrae. When will he come back?' Morel smiled conspiratorially. 'You are a magus as well,' he whispered. 'You have the power. I know that.'

Kathryn went cold but kept her face impassive. 'I don't know.' She patted Morel on the hand. 'But take comfort.'

'I'll be waiting,' Morel called as they walked towards the door. 'I trust you, Mistress Swinbrooke, as does my master.'

Kathryn closed her eyes, only opening them when Colum shut the door behind her. She took a deep breath and stared round the blighted garden.

'He's mad,' she whispered.

'But he believes,' Colum replied. He looped his arm gently through hers and led her out into Black Griffin Lane. 'Your hands are cold. Are you frightened, Kathryn? I certainly am!'

Kathryn forced a smile.

'Do you believe in Tenebrae's magic?' Colum asked.

'I believe,' Kathryn said, walking slowly down the street, still grasping Colum's hand, 'that there's more to our world, Irishman, than meets the eye. Powers of light as well as those of darkness. But magic?' She squeezed the Irishman's arm. 'Colum, God is my witness, I don't even know how the body works. Why does the blood flow round? How does the heart keep pumping? And the mind, the soul? Not to mention their sicknesses? It's what people believe.' She paused at a memory, then continued. 'Years ago, when I was a child, my father took me down to the Buttermarket. He wished to buy some herbs. We found the place all a-riot because a man had arrived dressed in goatskins, his skin burnt dark by the sun. He carried a staff in one hand and a bell in the other, and kept ringing this whilst screaming at the people to repent. He called himself Jonah. He believed he was the reincarnation of the prophet in the Bible and that Canterbury was Nineveh. Someone asked my father to cure the man.' She took a breath as they reached the entrance to the Bishop's Mitre. 'Do you know what my father replied? He said that if he believed he was Jonah and this Nineveh, not even an angel from heaven would dare contradict him.' She licked her lips, still dry after her visit to that hideous death chamber. 'That's the power of people like Tenebrae. They control the mind. They build strange worlds, people them with demons, goblins and sprites. May God help those who wander into such a world. They are locked in, unable to get out.'

Colum placed an arm round her shoulders and hugged her.

'You'd have made a fine priest, Kathryn. As they say in Ireland, you have the power of the words.'

'Aye, Colum Murtagh,' she retorted sharply. 'And you are the same. As Thomasina says, a teller of tales.'

Colum grinned. 'I was only praising you.'

'Flattery is like perfume,' Kathryn replied. 'You smell it, Irishman, but only a fool would drink it. Now come, we have people to question.'

46

They went down the passageway into the spacious taproom. Now mid-afternoon, the place was quiet though the air was still hot and stuffy with sweet smells of cooking and baking from the kitchen beyond. Hetherington had made his presence felt, commandeering a huge table near the one and only large window. The banker and his party had apparently dined well. The platters in front of them were littered with flagons, jugs, chicken bones, scraps of bread and vegetables. As Colum approached, Hetherington made no attempt to rise but, snapping his fingers, called over a limping, sweaty-faced tapster.

'Our guests,' he declared pompously. 'Two more stools, man!' He glared up at Colum. 'You wish some food?'

Kathryn took one look at the merchant's grease-stained mouth and decided her appetite could wait.

'Some wine perhaps. Mixed with water.'

'And I'll have a blackjack of ale,' Colum added.

He helped Kathryn onto the three-legged stool the scullion brought.

'Well?' Hetherington crossed fat fingers across his protuberant belly and leaned back in his chair. 'We have wasted considerable time. We had arranged a special visit to the Blessed Martyr's tomb.'

'Then why didn't you go?' Colum retorted, resentful at this merchant's arrogant ways.

'You asked us to stay.' Hetherington pursed his lips, his eyes rounded in anger.

'I asked you to stay,' Colum said, 'because you were waiting outside Tenebrae's house. And why should you go there?'

'Because,' Hetherington stammered. 'Because . . .'

Mistress Dauncey spoke up. 'Because we were the last to visit Tenebrae before . . .'

'Before his murder?' Colum finished, staring across at the ravaged beauty of the widow's face. 'And why should you do that?'

'We were worried.' Fronzac the clerk spoke up, wiping his greasy chin with the cuff of his jerkin. 'Master Tenebrae had powerful patrons.'

'Which one of you,' Kathryn intervened tactfully, 'was the last to see Tenebrae?'

'I was,' the widow Dauncey said. 'The porter Bogbean saw me leave.'

Kathryn made a note to hunt this strange-sounding porter down.

'He let me out. I returned to our tavern.'

'Which is?' Colum asked.

'The Kestrel, the other side of Westgate,' Hetherington said.

Kathryn was about to continue her questions when she noticed that the scullion who had brought the stools was still hovering, apparently interested in all that was being said. Fronzac followed her gaze and leaned over the table.

'Must we speak here?' he whispered hoarsely. 'Sir Raymond, we have been here for over an hour. The scullions and tapsters knew Tenebrae and, I believe, are now listening in on our every word.'

Kathryn stared round the tavern and, although only a few other people were there, she was forced to agree.

'We are holding a banquet tonight at the Kestrel,' Hetherington trumpeted. 'Mistress Swinbrooke, you and Master Murtagh will be our most welcome guests.'

His eyes twinkled with merriment, and Kathryn smiled back. Beneath his pomposity, Hetherington seemed a kind, affectionate man. She glanced at Colum, who nodded.

'We gratefully accept,' she replied. 'Though we would like to know more about you.'

'My business is in Cheapside,' Hetherington pronounced. 'And I am third guildmaster. It is my job to carry the silver mace in the procession and always sit to the right of the Chief Guildmaster at any banquet.'

Kathryn nudged Colum with her knee. The Irishman had an infectious sense of humour and, when he did laugh, found it difficult to stop. Hetherington beamed at Kathryn as if he fully expected her to be totally overcome by such a revelation.

'Sir Raymond,' Colum intervened. 'Your name is known here in Canterbury.'

Hetherington was flattered by the lie.

'This year it is my turn to visit the Blessed Shrine. Master Neverett here is my assistant. He has completed his articles and next year, God willing, might be admitted to full membership of the Guild.' He affectionately patted the young man on the shoulder. 'I have no son,' he said, leaning over the table. 'And Richard is God's consolation to me. Louise here,' he turned to his left, and a young woman simpered coyly up at him. 'Is my niece. She and Richard are betrothed and are to be married, just after May Day. Master Fronzac and Brissot are, of course, highly respected officers of the Guild. You, Mistress Swinbrooke, must have heard of physician Brissot's reputation? He has, on many occasions, quietened my own humours and made accurate predictions after studying my phlegm and urine.'

Hetherington stared suspiciously at Kathryn, who was now furiously chewing the corner of her lip.

'And I, too, am a member of the Guild,' Dionysia Dauncey intervened drily. She winked quickly at Kathryn. 'My husband died ten years ago. However, much to the surprise of many,' she glanced disparagingly at Hetherington, 'I managed to hold my own.'

'And how long have you been in Canterbury?' Kathryn asked.

'We arrived two days ago,' Hetherington replied. 'And we have seen all the sights. I have kissed the remains of Becket's shirt and visited the monks at Christchurch priory. We hope to begin our journey back to London tomorrow.'

'I am afraid not,' Colum spoke up, stilling the clamour with his hand. 'A crime has been committed within the jurisdiction of this city.'

'Are you accusing us?' Brissot snapped.

'We have business in London,' Neverett declared.

'If you left Canterbury,' Colum replied, 'some people might say you are fugitives. After all, you were the last to see Master Tenebrae alive.'

'It's best if you stay,' Kathryn insisted tactfully. 'If you return to London, others more harsh than Master Murtagh might take up his task. You have met the Queen's emissary Theobald Foliot?'

Hetherington nodded. 'Aye. A dark shadow that, Mistress Swinbrooke.' He wetted his fat lips. 'We will stay.' He concluded and made to rise but Kathryn gestured at him to remain seated.

'We will leave soon,' she said. 'One thing, however, does puzzle me.'

'Which is?' Fronzac asked.

'Well, you are all powerful members of a London Guild, prosperous men and women, loyal subjects of the kingdom and Holy Mother Church.' Kathryn deliberately emphasized the last three words.

'And so, what were we doing with the likes of Tenebrae?' Widow Dauncey asked.

'Precisely.'

'Oh, it's quite simple,' Hetherington explained. 'We are goldsmiths, Mistress Swinbrooke, and Fortune's fickle wheel often takes a sudden turn. We fashion and sell precious objects, but we also loan money.' He looked down at his podgy fingers spread out on the table-top and gave a loud sigh. 'The Civil War has ended.' He glanced up, his eyes cold and calculating. 'What happens, physician, to those goldsmiths who lent money to the House of Lancaster? And what for the future? The Lancastrian faction still survives, albeit in exile. We have the words of the Bible: "How a shrewd man always looks to the future and arranges his affairs accordingly".'

Kathryn knew enough about the great merchant princes to realise they calculated on who held power, whose star was in the ascendant and whose was about to fall. She also suspected that the likes of Hetherington and the rest might have a great deal to hide.

'And Tenebrae could see the future?' she asked.

Hetherington chuckled. 'Come, come, Mistress Swinbrooke, we are all hardheaded. To be sure Master Tenebrae had his gifts. More important, he had sharp ears: the tittle-tattle of court, the gossip from abroad, the scandals of Church and State.'

'He was also a blackmailer,' Colum declared.

Hetherington's face became grim.

'He knew secrets,' Kathryn said. 'Not only about those at court, but even perhaps the respectable members of a Guild.'

'Nonsense!' Neverett spluttered, lowering his cup.

Kathryn studied this arrogant young man, who had been staring at her disdainfully ever since they'd arrived.

'Are you so sure, Master Neverett?' Kathryn asked. 'Can you vouch that no one at this table has secrets to hide?'

Sir Raymond clapped his hands. 'Enough is enough. Mistress Swinbrooke, I will also send an invitation to Master Foliot to be our guest tonight. We have hired a private room at the Kestrel.'

'Yes,' Kathryn agreed, getting to her feet. 'It's best if such questions are asked then.'

'At which hour, Sir Raymond?'

'After Vespers, just as the cathedral bells finish tolling.'

Kathryn smiled her thanks. She and Colum made their farewells and they walked back to Black Griffin Lane.

'Well, my sharp-eyed healer,' Colum murmured. 'What do you make of those?'

'Wealthy and powerful,' Kathryn replied. 'They might have a great deal to hide.'

'And murder?'

'Perhaps.' She glanced up at Murtagh. 'Which begs other questions. First,' she continued. 'What did the grimoire hold? And, second, will its new owner use its secrets?'

'If she or he does,' Colum observed, 'I wager Tenebrae won't be the only one to die.'

They passed Tenebrae's house. Colum made to go on along Saint Peter's Street when Kathryn stopped and stared up at the dead magus's forbidding mansion.

'You are looking forward to tonight, Colum?'

'An evening with you?' Colum replied. 'Good food and wine: perhaps interesting company? Many men would regard that as heaven itself.'

'Flatterer,' Kathryn teased. She pulled him by the sleeve and pointed to the alley-way that ran alongside Tenebrae's mansion. 'Let's first search there.'

Colum followed her down the narrow, evil-smelling runnel, not more than two yards wide. On their left rose the wall of the next house, nothing but timber and plaster, on their right the wall of Tenebrae's mansion. Kathryn paused at the corner of the alley-way and pointed up to the shuttered window.

'That's the one we examined on the gallery.'

They continued round the back of the house, noting the door and the wooden outside steps leading down.

'Each of Hetherington's party left, using this,' Kathryn explained.

She stared at the heaps of rubbish piled in the alley-way: scraps of rag, the decomposing contents of night-jars, bits of mouldering food, scraps of parchment.

'Tenebrae must have used this as his midden-heap,' Kathryn exclaimed, pinching her nostrils against the smell.

They continued round the alley-way. Kathryn, looking up, noticed the shuttered window on the second floor.

'Tenebrae's chamber,' she declared. 'It looks as if Morel has closed the shutters.'

'I can see no other entrance,' Colum said.

They went back into Black Griffin Lane. The one-eyed tinker was still on the corner bawling hoarsely.

'A few needles! A few needles and threads for sale! Ribbons and bows!' He waved Colum over and picked up a scrap of pink silk. 'For your lady, Master? It will make a nice bow. Or perhaps a brooch?'

Colum was about to shake his head and pass on. Kathryn, however, took the pink ribbon from the man's hand and gave him a penny. The tinker's dirty face broke into a grin.

'Come back tomorrow.'

'First,' Kathryn pointed to the sore on the man's dirty fingers, 'buy some fig wort or bethany mixed with water and your chilblains will disappear.'

The tinker stared at her curiously. 'I can't buy that!'

Kathryn passed another penny across. 'Come to my house in Ottemelle Lane. Ask for Thomasina. She will give it to you free. But that's for your belly: buy some hot broth.'

'And what do you want?' the tinker asked suspiciously.

'The whereabouts of Master Bogbean?'

The tinker gave his gap-toothed smile and pointed to a small, dingy ale house.

'You'll find him in there, drunk as a fart. Bogbean has two homes. That alehouse, where he cleans the pots probably in his own urine, so I wouldn't touch a drop, and the alley-way behind the magus's house. Buy him a drink and he'll tell you everything. Buy him two and he's yours for life!'

Kathryn thanked him. Both she and Colum entered the dingy alehouse, nothing more than a low timbered shed, with one narrow window, a few rickety tables and small tuns serving as stools. The shabbily dressed customers looked up as they entered.

'Bogbean!' Colum shouted. 'I wish to buy Bogbean a drink!'

A shabby, fat man rose from his stool where he had sat slouched tipsily against the wall and staggered towards them. Kathryn gazed at him in astonishment: small and squat, he had a face as round and red as a berry, blue veins high in his cheeks and a fiery nose, which declared him to be a toper born and bred. However, it was his hair which made Kathryn gape. Black and greasy, it stood up from his head like a cluster of spikes.

'Bogbean's the name,' he slurred. 'And what, shir, can I do for you?'

'An answer to some questions.' Colum pressed a coin into the man's hard, calloused hand.

Bogbean stared back and gave a lopsided grin. He swayed dangerously on his feet as if the floor of the alehouse was the deck of a ship.

'Ask your questions,' the fellow breathed, leering at Kathryn, 'and I'll give you honest answers. But for God's sake sit down!' He blinked wearily around. 'This bloody place is beginning to move!'

Kathryn, hiding her giggles, sat down at the slop-stained table. She felt rather precarious on the small tun. Bogbean shouted at a thin-faced slattern and the girl brought over blackjacks popping with ale. Kathryn remembered the tinker's advice: she refused to touch the tankard. Bogbean finished his drink and started on hers.

'Well.' He smacked froth-rimmed lips. 'Ask your questions.'

'You worked for Tenebrae?'

'Aye, the evil bastard's dead. And worse, Bogbean is out of office.'

'What was your office?' Kathryn asked.

'Porter to the back chamber,' Bogbean pompously announced. 'Whenever Master Tenebrae had guests.' He leaned closer. 'And believe me, Mistress, he had guests! The great and the mighty, Princes of the Church.' He winked slowly and tapped the side of his fleshy nose. 'What Bogbean sees, Bogbean never forgets!'

'And what were your duties?' Kathryn asked.

'I guarded the door. No one went in.' He slurped again from

his tankard. 'Well, no one could go in. However, no one came out without Bogbean's knowledge.'

'And this morning?'

'Well, it was raining heavily. Sir Raymond Hetherington's party came. Morel told me about them.' Bogbean leaned back in his chair, his eyes narrowed. 'You have met Morel?' He shook his head. 'As strange as his master: he's a few pennies short of a shilling is old Morel.'

'Sir Raymond Hetherington?' Colum insisted.

'Oh aye, the goldsmith. They all came down: Hetherington first, Neverett, Condosti, Brissot, Fronzac and Greene. Finally, that old widow, I forget her name.' He tapped his head. 'My brain's going soft. Ah, yes, Dauncey.'

'How do you know all their names?'

Bogbean brought a dirty scrap of parchment from the inside of his even dirtier cuff and laid it on the table.

'May we have that?' Kathryn asked, examining it closely.

'It's a list of names,' Bogbean explained. 'And I can read. When I was a boy I went to the cathedral school. Master Tenebrae always gave me a list of who were visiting him and in what order.'

'And this is the list?' Kathryn asked.

'Oh, yes.'

'And how were they?' Kathryn asked.

Bogbean shrugged. 'They all came tripping out. Never spoke a word, except that old one, Dauncey: she smiled and gave me a coin. She dropped her purse. I helped pick up the pennies. She thanked me and said I would see her again, God willing, next year.'

'And nothing else?'

Bogbean shook his head. 'No. Why, should there be?'

'Did anyone go in through that door?' Colum asked.

Bogbean shook his head. 'Not a mouse, not a sparrow. Master

Tenebrae was a hard taskmaster. If I'd left, even for a piss, he'd have taken my head!'

Colum put a coin on the table.

They left the alehouse and walked back into Saint Peter's Lane, unaware of Morel standing in the shadowy corner of a shop, greedily watching Kathryn's retreating back.

Chapter 4

Kathryn and Colum returned to Ottemelle Lane. The Irishman decided it was too late to go out to Kingsmead.

'Holbech,' he said, referring to his lieutenant, 'will take care of everything.' He chewed his lip. 'Yet there are accounts to be drawn up; the Exchequer will need them by Lady's Day.'

Kathryn, too, became busy as a number of patients arrived: first, Rawnose the beggar suffering from a scabied head, though his tongue was as busy as ever. He insisted on telling Kathryn the gossip of the city.

'There's fairies been glimpsed in Bean Wood dancing round the upright stone. A two-headed lamb was born at a farm near Maidstone. They say the King is going to declare war on the French and his Commissioners will soon be looking for troops. . . .'

Kathryn half listened as Rawnose prattled on. At last she sent him away happy, having rubbed some peterswort into his scalp. Mollyns the baker arrived next, complaining of a sour mouth and left with a concoction of ale hoop. Peterkin the butcher with a cut on his wrist was also waiting. Kathryn made up a poultice whilst

Thomasina loudly scolded the fellow for not being more careful with his knives.

Kathryn found it difficult to concentrate. She kept remembering that sombre chamber and Tenebrae's body slumped there. How was he murdered? Kathryn wondered. No one forced their way in yet the magus was alive when Morel came up after all the visitors had left.

'You are day-dreaming!' Thomasina snapped. 'Not about the Irishman again, surely? He'll addle your wits! I remember what my father said about Irishmen. . . .'

'Thomasina! I know only too well what your father said about Irishmen.'

'Well, he should know,' Thomasina replied. 'He was Irish himself.'

Kathryn started. 'I never knew that, Thomasina.'

'Oh, yes, for a few years he was in service with the Duke of Cambridge. He served in France as an archer.'

Thomasina was about to continue her family history when there was a knock on the door and an old, bent, white-haired man shuffled in.

'Oh, it's Jack-by-the-Hedge!' Thomasina cried.

She helped the visitor to a stool by the table. Jack threw her a toothless smile, his rheumy eyes twinkling with pleasure.

'Thomasina, you are as plump and happy as ever? A toothsome piece between the sheets, eh?'

Thomasina slapped the old man playfully on the hand as Kathryn crouched down before him. She never knew his real name, but Jack-by-the-Hedge was what everyone called him, because he lived in a hut of mud and wattle out in the fields near the Stour.

'What's wrong, Jack?' Kathryn asked.

'I have a pain,' the old man said. He opened his mouth and pulled up his dry lip to show the inflamed gums. 'I thought it would go away. Always hurt me it has. When I followed King Hal to Agincourt my gums hurt as if I was in hell.'

Kathryn smiled at this old man. No one really knew his age but he claimed to have been a boy when King Henry V fought at Agincourt in 1415 and slaughtered the French. Kathryn gave him some rose-hip syrup, an astringent made from wild briar, as well as a small piece of cotton to dab it on his gums. She looked into his wily, old eyes.

'You are not really here for your gums, Jack?'

'They haven't paid me my pension,' the old man replied. 'The monks of Christchurch. My pension is my right.' He took out a battered piece of vellum with an ancient seal appended to it. 'Three shillings to be given every quarter. The crafty buggers pretend I'm dead.'

Kathryn slipped a coin into the old man's hand.

'Take the rose-hip, Jack. Thomasina will wrap you some food. Tomorrow, I promise, Thomasina will go and see the Prior of Christchurch.'

'Aye,' the nurse retorted. 'I'll tell that shaven-head, mealy-mouthed almoner to open his coffers. Then I'll come and see you, Jack my boy. Make sure you have wood and kindling for a fire.'

'If you stayed,' Jack whispered, 'I'd be warm enough.'

'Shame on you!' Thomasina cried in mock horror.

Kathryn moved away as Wuf danced into the kitchen. Whilst Thomasina prepared the food, the boy took Jack out into the garden to listen, once more, to the old man's famous exploits.

Darkness was beginning to fall so Kathryn returned to her own chamber where she washed and changed into her best gown of tawny sarcanet fringed at the cuff and neck with white linen. She sat on the bed combing her hair, wondering what she'd discover at the pilgrims' supper. Colum tapped on the door and said he was ready.

'I'll be down soon,' Kathryn cried absentmindedly.

She put on woollen hose, made sure her kirtle hung properly and applied some paint to her face. 'Gilding the lily' as Colum called it. She caught up her hair, put on a dark blue wimple and took out a soft pair of leather boots from her aumbry. Colum was waiting for her in the kitchen. He was dressed in a dark doublet, matching hose and leather riding boots. He had his silver chain of office round his neck as if to remind those powerful goldsmiths of his position; his great leather war belt was slung over his shoulder. When he saw Kathryn, he ran his hands round his cheeks and chin.

'Before you ask, Mistress, I have bathed and shaved.' He patted his hair. 'I have even combed my golden locks.'

'Which just goes to prove,' Thomasina snapped, 'you can't make a silk purse out of a sow's ear!'

Colum laughed.

'Has Jack-by-the-Hedge left?' Kathryn asked before Thomasina could continue her verbal assault.

'Oh, yes, trotted off happy as a squirrel.'

Kathryn sat down beside Colum.

'Is that necessary?' she asked, pointing to the war belt with its sword and dagger sheathed.

'Canterbury is dangerous now,' Colum replied. 'Where there are pilgrims there are thieves, pickpockets and gangs of rifflers who'd cut a child's throat for a penny.'

Kathryn was about to demur when there was a knock on the door. Agnes answered and Kathryn pulled a face as she recognised Foliot's voice. He strode into the kitchen dressed in his usual black garb, as if he could not be bothered to make any pretence at dressing for the occasion.

'I heard you had received an invitation,' he said, kissing Kathryn's hand as she rose to greet him. He bowed civilly at Colum. 'So I thought we'd arrive together.' He tapped the toe of his boot against the floor and stared around. 'Your fame as a physician, Mistress Swinbrooke, has gone before you. It must be pleasant to have a home, a place you can retreat to.'

'And you have none?' Kathryn asked.

Foliot smiled and pointed at Colum. 'Ask the Irishman. At

court there's no place to hide. Ah, well.' He paused as the great bells of the cathedral began to chime. 'Our hosts will be waiting.'

Colum, not pleased at his arrival, muttered that he would collect their horses. Kathryn made her farewells and led Foliot out into the street. Colum returned with their mounts from stables at a nearby tavern. Foliot gallantly assisted Kathryn mount and, with Colum riding alongside, they made their way down Ottemelle Lane and into Saint Margaret's Street. Colum sat on his horse, back rigid, whilst Kathryn found Foliot's silence embarrassing. She leaned over.

'Do you know any of the goldsmiths?'

'No, Mistress, but I know of them: I recognise their type: rich and powerful, fertile ground for the likes of Tenebrae. You see, bankers and goldsmiths like power. They prefer stability but, during the Civil War, they did not have that. Consequently they entered into negotiations and made shadowy alliances with every party. Now they are frightened that their secret sins will be made public.'

'And Tenebrae would know their secrets?'

'Possibly. As well as the scandals of their private or family lives. I wager you a pair of the best kid gloves, Mistress Swinbrooke, that Tenebrae was murdered because of his greed for power and riches.'

'As Chaucer's Pardoner would say,' Colum called over his shoulder, ' "The love of wealth is the root of all evil".'

'You know Chaucer, Irishman?'

Colum pulled his horse back. 'I have read his *Canterbury Tales.*'

'My grandfather knew him,' Foliot replied. 'The poet worked in the Custom House when he was an apprentice clerk.'

Kathryn hid her smile. Foliot had hit his mark and won Colum's attention. Both men began to discuss heatedly which was the best story and whether the Tales were superior to Chaucer's *Parliament of Foules* or *The Book of the Duchess*. As they talked Kathryn patted her horse's neck; sometimes she found Colum's constant quotations from Chaucer exasperating; now she was glad he was distracted.

She looked round Saint Margaret's Street. The pilgrims were now flocking back to the taverns and guest houses, all chattering volubly. Some were local people, others from the shires even north of the Trent. A few, with their broad-brimmed hats, staves and scallop-shell badges, proclaimed them to be professional pilgrims who visited the tombs of Saint Ursula in Cologne or Saint James at Compostella.

The tradesmen had put away their stalls. Only a few pedlars and scrawny-armed beggars still looked for trade. As they passed the Bullstake and entered the Buttermarket in Burghgate, a small crowd had gathered to watch a mad beggar woman dance above a heap of glowing charcoal, which had been tipped from a brazier. The poor woman danced for a while, but then the pain became too intense and she had to run to a horse trough to cool her scorched feet. Kathryn would have stopped, but Foliot looked back at her.

'It's a cruel world, Mistress Swinbrooke. There is nothing we can do!'

A passing friar stopped to help the madwoman. Kathryn rode on down Burghgate and into the great cobbled yard of the Kestrel tavern. A large, prosperous tavern, the Kestrel's lower storey was made of red brick, the three upper tiers of gleaming pink plaster and shiny black beams under broad, wooden eaves. The casement windows were of mullioned glass, some even tinted and coloured. Smartly painted stables and outhouses stood around the wall, with grooms and ostlers busy feeding the horses and settling them for the night. They dismounted, gave their reins to the waiting grooms and entered the spacious hallway of scrubbed, honey-coloured sandstone, its plaster and woodwork freshly painted. Sir Raymond Hetherington and the rest of the pilgrims were seated at a window table in the spacious taproom. They were dressed in their finery, and their flushed faces and glittering eyes, the high-pitched chatter of their conversation, showed all had drunk well and deep. Colum apologised for being late but Hetherington brushed this aside.

'You are most welcome, most welcome!'

And without further ado, Hetherington led them all up the broad, sweeping staircase to a specially hired room on the second floor. The walls were wainscoted with gleaming, dark brown oak. A small fire burnt in the hearth. A long trestle table had been set up down the centre of the room and covered in gold-fringed, cream-coloured linen cloths. Cresset torches flared and sputtered on the walls above the wainscoting. Beeswax candles and oil lamps were set along the table. Hetherington showed them to their seats: Kathryn to his right, Colum and Foliot to his left, the rest of the guests taking their places according to precedence with Fronzac and Brissot seated below the burnished silver salt cellar carved in the shape of a ship. Supper was briskly served; cheese tart, mushroom pasties, cream soup of pork, chicken in rose-water, goose, roast pheasant and capons in a pepper sauce. The landlord, with an eye to a large profit, had the servitors and tapsters running backwards and forwards. For a while the conversation was mundane though Brissot, much the worse for drink and eager to impress Kathryn, gave his companions a lecture on the virtues of sage.

'It's grown under the influence of Jupiter,' he trumpeted. 'It's good for the liver and the blood. It provokes urine, cleans stomach ulcers and cures the spitting and casting of blood.'

Kathryn glanced down the table and nodded knowingly. Foliot seized the embarrassed silence to tap his silver-edged pewter spoon on the table.

'Sir Raymond, we thank you for your hospitality.' He winked mischievously at Kathryn who had eaten little and drunk even less. 'But we must question you all on Tenebrae's death.'

He paused to sip from his cup. Kathryn sensed the change of atmosphere in the room. If these powerful people had hoped that

Tenebrae's death was a momentary wonder, then they were to be sorely disappointed.

'You each saw Tenebrae between the hours of nine and noon?' Foliot continued. 'And, unless I have it wrong, Sir Raymond, you went first?'

The fat goldsmith burped in agreement.

'Then Neverett, the lovely Mistress Condosti, then me and Fronzac!' Brissot bellowed louder than he intended, 'And finally Master Greene and Widow Dauncey.'

A chorus of agreement greeted his words.

'Are you sure that it was Tenebrae you saw?'

'Of course!' Greene snapped, his face as sour as vinegar. 'What do you think we are, Mistress, bumpkins?'

His words provoked a ripple of mirth.

'And who decided on that order?' Kathryn asked.

'Well, we all did,' Neverett intervened. 'When we arrived in Canterbury Master Fronzac, our clerk, asked about our arrangements, then went to see Tenebrae. Each of us was given about the same amount of time, about twenty minutes with short intervals in between. And the cost was the same, a silver piece at least.'

'And how did Master Tenebrae conduct these meetings?' Kathryn asked.

'Well you have seen the room,' Louise Condosti simpered. 'Sometimes it could be quite frightening. Master Morel would take us up the stairs and knock three times.' She smiled. 'Always the same: Tenebrae would ask who it was and Morel would reply, "A seeker of the truth".'

'Then what?' Colum asked, intrigued by how these rich, sophisticated people could be so gullible.

'It depends on your circumstances,' Widow Dauncey snapped. 'I sat on the stool before Master Tenebrae. There were a few questions, courtesies, but then I'd ask my questions.'

'Which were?' Kathryn insisted.

The widow breathed in so deeply her nostrils flared in annoyance.

'Is this really necessary?' she asked quietly. Glimpsing Foliot's grimace of annoyance, she sighed. 'If you insist. They were questions anyone would ask such a man: the future . . .' Dauncey paused and Kathryn knew she was being very careful. Any questions about the stability of the Crown or the health of the King could be construed as treason. Dauncey hid her confusion by sipping from her goblet. 'Which markets would prosper,' she added hastily. 'What dangers I might face?'

'And how did Tenebrae answer these?'

'By use of the tarot cards: the ace of coins for happiness; the five of swords means a loss; the three of coins, trade; the five of clubs, a lawsuit.' Dauncey shrugged.

'And what does the future hold for you?' Colum asked.

'Prosperity!'

'And the same is true of all of you?' Foliot demanded.

'There's always danger,' Hetherington snapped.

'And the grimoire?' Kathryn watched the pilgrims tense. 'How did Tenebrae use the grimoire of Honorius?'

'He would read from it,' Greene spoke up. 'Chant an incantation before the cards were turned.'

Kathryn glanced quickly at Colum. They are lying, her look said, we will never get the truth from them.

'What was the grimoire like?' Colum asked.

'About the size of a church missal, studded with strange gems bound in what looked like calfskin,' Greene replied.

'And so you all went to see Master Tenebrae at your appointed time?' Kathryn asked.

'Yes,' Neverett replied. 'As Widow Dauncey said. We sat before the table. Tenebrae was always clothed in black, his mask and hood over his face. He spoke softly but deeply: no real chatter, no wine was offered or taken. Tenebrae let me out by the rear door, into the small gallery and down the stairs to the doorway leading into the alley where that creature, Bogbean, was waiting.' Neverett laughed nervously. 'Tenebrae always insisted on that: those coming to seek his wisdom would never meet those leaving.'

'And did you believe all his wisdom?' Kathryn asked. She glanced round the company. 'Powerful goldsmiths! Didn't it ever occur to you that Tenebrae was a spy with fingers in pies up and down the kingdom? That he acquired knowledge and used it under the guise of magic?'

'If it was wrong,' Hetherington asked, 'why wasn't Tenebrae arrested? I believe, Master Foliot, even Her Grace the Queen, may God bless her, had dealings with the magus.'

'Her Grace's dealings in this matter,' Foliot retorted, 'are not for common chatter or vulgar report.'

'Well,' Hetherington snapped, his face now flushed, 'then our dealings, sir, are our own business! Yes, we visited Tenebrae but there's no crime in that. We may have been the last to see him, but is that proof of murder? You have seen his servant Morel. He is as capable of murder as anyone. And how do we know, Master Foliot, what was said when you visited him earlier in the day? You did visit him, didn't you?'

For the first time ever, the Queen's emissary lost some of his poise. Foliot opened his mouth to reply but then thought better of it.

'Come, come!' Brissot piped up. 'Master Tenebrae was a powerful man and he had his enemies.' He smiled patronisingly. 'And I am sure the truth will soon come out.' He stretched and yawned. 'But the evening is drawing on. Perhaps if we took our wine out into the gardens beyond?'

Everyone quickly agreed. The atmosphere in the room was becoming oppressive, tempers were fraying. They picked up their goblets and went down the stairs, through the deserted taproom where heavy-eyed scullions were now preparing for sleep on straw-filled mattresses. Outside, behind the tavern, was a small, cobbled yard bounded by a fence with a small, wicket gate. The night air was cool and refreshing after the hot, stuffy banqueting room. Kathryn looked up and marvelled at the stars filling the dark sky with light. They went through the gate, past the herb gardens where Kathryn smelt the fragrance of balm, parsley, rosemary, yarrow, then further down past the hen coops and dovecotes. She stopped abruptly, wrinkling her nose at the pungent smell. Brissot, walking beside her and regaling her with a list of miraculous cures, paused in his monologue. Foliot, too, exclaimed and pinched his nostrils whilst Colum just laughed.

'Haven't you ever smelt hogs before?' the Irishman asked.

'The tavern has its own farm,' Fronzac explained and pointed to a small paddock cordoned off by a high fence.

Kathryn heard the grunting, shuffling and pushing of the hogs within. Colum, full of mischief, seized her by the elbow.

'Come on, Kathryn,' he whispered. 'In Ireland these creatures proved great sport.'

And with Fronzac and Foliot following, the rest staying behind, Colum guided her to the fence and onto a stump of a tree placed there. Kathryn, full of curiosity, climbed up and looked over. She glimpsed a sea of angry eyes and bristling snouts, tufted ears, fat bellies and tails high in anger. She hurriedly got down.

'Sport, Irishman?'

In the darkness, Colum's smile widened.

'My father had a small farm,' he said. 'Now and again for mischief we let such creatures out. They are not pigs; hogs are fierce and will bite. You have to run like the wind to escape them.'

Kathryn walked back to join the rest. Louise Condosti, a napkin covering her mouth and nose, was leaning coyly against her betrothed.

'I can't stand such animals.'

'Fronzac is fascinated by them,' Greene taunted acidly.

'My father owned a tavern like this,' the clerk said. 'Near Mapledurham on the old road west. I could sit for hours and watch them eating.'

'Is that to be our only pastime?' Hetherington trumpeted, confronting Colum and Foliot. 'How long, sir, must we stay in Canterbury?'

Colum glanced at the Queen's emissary.

'Today is Tuesday,' Foliot replied slowly. 'If Tenebrae's death remains a mystery by the end of the week, then you may go.' He held up a hand to still their protests. 'But, once you are back in London, the King's Justices will deal with the matter.'

After that, Colum, Foliot and Kathryn made their farewells. Kathryn had the distinct impression that the pilgrims were pleased to see the back of them. They mounted their horses and rode back into a moonlit Burghgate. The houses were now shuttered, the thoroughfare deserted except for the occasional wandering cat or beggar whining for alms from the darkness.

They rode silently down into Saint Margaret's Street where Foliot reined in and turned his horse.

'Well,' he asked, 'What do you make of all that?'

'They are lying,' Kathryn said. 'They believed in the magus. Oh, not because he was a magician but because he was a collector of information, a snapper-up of facts, tittle-tattle and gossip.'

Foliot nodded. 'I agree. That's how such men work. You go to them and, on the first occasion, receive sweet blandishments. However, once they have your name and status, they make enquiries, collect information. Tenebrae was no different.'

'Do you think the murderer is one of them?' Colum asked.

Kathryn replied carefully, 'What happens if all of them murdered Tenebrae?'

Colum stared up between the overhanging houses at the starlit sky.

'But Morel went up afterwards: he spoke to his master.'

Kathryn shook her head. 'How do we know that to be true?

Tenebrae was dressed in black, hooded and masked: any one of those merchants could have imitated his voice.'

Foliot laughed. 'You are too sharp, Mistress Swinbrooke.'

'To answer your question, Colum,' Kathryn added bluntly, 'I still believe one, or all of them killed Tenebrae: how or when is a mystery. Beneath the wine, the good food and courtesies there is a tension, a watchfulness. They do not trust each other.'

'So, how do we proceed?' Foliot asked. 'I could go back to that tavern and tear it apart until I find the grimoire.'

Kathryn shook her head. 'The Book of Shadows will be hidden.' She chewed the corner of her lip. 'No, what we must do is find the loose thread. Jerk it sharply and the truth will unravel.'

'Then do it soon.' Foliot gathered the reins in his hand. He leaned over and grasped Kathryn's hand. 'If I go back to London with the grimoire you will be Her Grace's friend for life but . . .'

'But what, sir?' Kathryn snapped. 'Are you threatening me?'

In the light of a torch burning in its sconce on the doorpost of a nearby house, Kathryn glimpsed a sad softness in Foliot's face.

'I'll never threaten you,' he promised. 'But the Queen will. Tell me, Mistress Swinbrooke, how would Canterbury be for you if Master Murtagh were recalled to London?'

Foliot did not wait to see the effect of his words, but spurred his horse back towards Queningate. Kathryn watched his retreating back whilst her stomach clenched and her mouth went dry.

'Could they do that?' she murmured.

Colum stared grimly back.

'Answer me!' she cried. 'Could they do that?'

Colum wrapped the reins of his horse round his hand.

'After the battle of Tewkesbury,' he said, 'the King granted me these offices for life. However, it wouldn't be the first time such a grant has been cancelled or revoked.'

'And would you go back?' Kathryn was now no longer aware of the darkened street or Tenebrae's death.

Colum smiled. ' "To love my lady",' he quoted from Chaucer's Knight, ' "Whom I love and serve and will, while life, my heart's blood shall preserve".'

'Don't play games with me, Irishman!'

Colum's face became grave. 'I am not. I have given you my answer. Foliot and his mistress can go hang.' He grasped the reins of Kathryn's horse and urged their mounts forward. 'What I'll do,' he added, 'is set up shop in Canterbury and sell physic.'

Kathryn glared at him. She still felt cold after Foliot's threat. She was angry that his words could be so cutting, but then she recalled the sadness in his eyes and recognised that Foliot was secretly warning her.

'Do you think there's a solution?' Colum asked.

'For every illness there's a cure,' she answered tartly. 'Apart from one.'

'Which is?'

'A broken heart!'

Kathryn urged her horse on, not caring about the tavern signs and ale-stakes jutting over the street. They turned into Ottemelle Lane. Kathryn dismounted, tossed the reins at Colum and, whilst he took the mounts back to the stables, she walked into the kitchen.

Thomasina was dozing in a chair in the ingle-nook. She woke with a start and would have fussed around but Kathryn insisted she retire.

'Not before that bloody Irishman, I won't!' Thomasina muttered. 'I know his likes, full of wine and it's heigh, nonny no!'

'Thomasina!'

The nurse stared across at Kathryn's pale face, the set to her mouth and jaw, the furrows round her eyes.

'I'm going to bed, Mistress,' Thomasina said quietly, 'and I think you should too.' She walked over and grasped Kathryn's hands. 'It is the Irishman?'

Kathryn nodded. 'They might recall him to London.'

'Nonsense!' Thomasina replied. 'Come, Kathryn, let the Irishman earn his keep. I'll lock and bolt the house. Go to bed, don't worry: as they say in Ireland, "We'll burn that bridge when we come to it".'

In Tenebrae's sombre, magic chamber, Morel, too, was sleepless. He sat on a stool staring across at the chair in which he had found his murdered master. Morel tried to make sense of what was happening to his world. Tenebrae had been a harsh master but Morel's only one. Many years ago, when he had been regarded as a monster in a travelling troupe of mountebanks and mummers, Tenebrae had bought him out. Oh, Tenebrae had beaten, frightened and even terrified him. However, the magus had put clothes on Morel's back and food in his belly. He had given Morel a soft bed with a feather-filled bolster, cupboards and chests as well as purses full of coins. Morel had been happy, sheltering like a bat in the shadow of Tenebrae's greatness. Now his master was gone. Morel could not understand that: his master could not die! To be sure, he had seen the bolt in Tenebrae's throat and the great Book of Shadows had disappeared but, surely, this was all part of some secret plan? Had not his master said,

'Morel, I can come and go as I will, even harrow the Valley of Death yet still return!'

Morel stared at the empty chair and listened to the creaking of the house. He always thought it strange. Tenebrae had no pets, no cat, no dog, but never once in all the years they had spent in this house had Morel even glimpsed a mouse, a rat or even a spider scurrying about.

'Where are you, Master?' he whispered into the darkness.

As if in answer, the old screech owl, which came in to hunt along the alley hooted mournfully. Morel sighed. Was that his answer? The master would return! But would he need assistance? Would he need Morel's help? The manservant became excited. And, when Tenebrae did return, perhaps the magus would reward him? Provide a feast? Perhaps give him coins? Or even, as he sometimes had, would he hire a whore for Morel then watch them cavort on his bed in the chamber above: some fresh, plump girl. Morel licked his lips. He was confused about how his master had died. He had been certain that each of Tenebrae's guests from the goldsmiths' fraternity had been shown up and then dismissed. Bogbean had said the same. Morel had helped Bogbean remember by squeezing his throat tightly in his hand until the porter, mottle-faced, popping-eyed and gasping for breath, had assured Morel that no trickery had taken place. There were no secret entrances or passageways into the house so Morel now believed that Tenebrae had arranged his own death for his own special purposes. The manservant shifted on his stool and stared up at the red, painted goat on the ceiling. And the others? The Irishman with his hands restless on his dagger hilt? And that sharpeyed Foliot, fresh from the court? Morel grunted disdainfully. But Mistress Swinbrooke? Morel narrowed his eyes, rocking himself gently backwards and forwards. Swinbrooke was cunning: she had the power. She would help him bring Master Tenebrae back.

Chapter 5

Kathryn woke early after a poor night's sleep. She had tossed and turned, fearful of Foliot's threat, as well as trying to imagine what could have happened the morning Tenebrae had died. She sat up and leaned against the bolsters. She closed her eyes and recalled that sombre staircase leading up to the magus's chamber. Morel would knock: Tenebrae would open the door and the visitor would go in. Once the meeting was over Tenebrae would show them out through the rear door. He or she would go past the shuttered window and down those stairs. Once out, both the door itself as well as Bogbean would ensure no one could re-enter. Try as she might, Kathryn could see no solution to the mystery. She beat her fists against the coverlets piled around her.

'One of those pilgrims,' she whispered to herself, 'is the assassin.'

She knew the dangers of brooding so she got out of bed, washed and dressed quickly, then went down to the kitchen where Thomasina was already building the fire in the grate. She broke her fast on some cheese, fruit and yesterday's bread, muttering answers to Thomasina's sharp questions.

'Are there any patients this morning?' Kathryn asked, trying to remember. 'I mean, anything serious?'

Before Thomasina answered there was a loud knocking on the door. Thomasina went to answer and came back.

'It's one of those arrogant tipstaffs from the Guildhall,' she announced. 'Grand Master Luberon would like to have words with you. I can't see why he doesn't come here. You are just as busy . . .'

'Shush!' Kathryn smiled. 'Colum has left?'

'Flown like a bird,' Thomasina replied. 'He looked about as happy as you. Shall I come?'

Kathryn shook her head, collected her cloak and, kissing Thomasina absentmindedly on the cheek, walked out into Ottemelle Lane.

Widow Gumple went sailing by, a false smile on her face. Kathryn nodded at this self-righteous, powerful member of Saint Mildred's parish council. She wished the woman would not make such a fool of herself by parading the streets in her voluminous skirts, which made her sway like a sumpter pony whilst her ornate head-dress billowed out like a ship in full sail.

'You are getting like Thomasina,' Kathryn whispered.

Rawnose the beggar was standing on the corner of Hethenman Lane. He beckoned her over and showed her his scabied head.

'It's working,' he gabbled, his poor, disfigured face breaking into a smile. 'It's magic. You work magic, Mistress Swinbrooke.'

Kathryn went to walk on, but Rawnose caught her by the hand.

'And you've heard about Master Tenebrae's death?' This self-proclaimed herald of Canterbury pursed his lips and shook his head as if he was one of the King's Justices. 'The demons are all about us. Have you heard about the curate at Maidstone who tried to kill the archdeacon with a waxen image? He pierced it with pins and threw it into a fire. He's supposed to keep by him in a bottle, a demon which spies on young girls of the parish. But that's nothing,' Rawnose chattered on, 'compared to an alderman in Dover. He bought three wax images and a supply of poison from a sorcerer. The images were baptised with the names of the sheriff and two leading civic officers, wrapped in strips of parchment and concealed with the poison in loaves of bread which were smuggled into the Guildhall. And have you heard . . . ?'

'Enough,' Kathryn interrupted. 'Rawnose, my medicine may have cured your head but, God save us, your tongue is getting longer. Now, go and see Thomasina. Tell her I sent you. You can break your fast there and warm yourself by the fire.'

The words were hardly out of her mouth when Rawnose was off like a hare. Kathryn continued up Hethenman Lane. The day was proving to be a fine one, the sun growing stronger in a cloud-free sky. Bells of different churches tolled for Mass. Carts crashed along the cobbles laden with produce for the markets. Two one-armed beggars pushed their common barrow laden with polished small stones, which they hoped to sell. Behind them a dusty friar prayed his beads. A group of pilgrims tried to ask the way from a tired, white-faced whore hurrying back towards her brothel in Westgate. On either side of the street, traders and merchants were laying out their stalls, smelly night-pots were being emptied into the streets whilst straggly children screamed with delight as the contents of one jar splattered a pompous-looking merchant. Kathryn espied Goldere the clerk clawing at his protuberant cod-piece and staring miserably around. She took a shortcut through an alley-way; Goldere, with his lists of intermittent ailments, which he was ever ready to describe in great detail to Kathryn, was more than she could take. As she entered the High Street Kathryn found the traders quiet, the main thoroughfare cleared of pilgrims, even the wandering dogs and pigs had been shooed away.

'It's the King's Justices in Eyre,' a woman whispered to her. 'They have arrived in Canterbury.'

Kathryn waited for a while as this great judicial procession made its way from the Guildhall to the castle. First came two heralds carrying large banners bearing the royal arms of England. They rode brown-berried palfreys, looking magnificent in their tabards of blue, red and gold. After them walked two tipstaffs carrying white wands, followed by a trumpeter and four pages beating solemnly on tambours almost as big as them. Then came the Justices dressed in their scarlet, ermine-edged cloaks and black skull caps; they were surrounded by their clerks, scriveners and finally the cart that struck dread in the eyes of all the spectators. It was high-sided, pulled by two huge dray horses, their manes hogged, their trappings all black. On the cart stood the executioner dressed from head to toe in black and red, his face disguised by a mask. Beside him were piled the implements of torture and punishment: a makeshift gallows, the block, axe and sword, pincers, irons and manacles. The Justices would spend at least two weeks in Canterbury thoroughly investigating all the cases brought before them. Men and women would be hanged, flogged, branded, mutilated or fined according to the whim of those gentle-faced old men swathed in their scarlet robes. Kathryn suddenly remembered the accused witch Mathilda Sempler and vowed to have words with Luberon. Once the Justices were passed and the High Street re-opened, she hastened to the Guildhall and was surprised to find Luberon waiting for her on the steps. Kathryn brushed the hair from her face.

'I'm sorry,' she gasped. 'But . . .'

The little clerk's eyes lit with pleasure. He grasped Kathryn's hands and blushed as she kissed him on his cheek. He fairly skipped as he led her along the smelly Guildhall passageway to his own chamber. Every available space and shelf in the whitewashed room was taken up with piles of manuscripts. Luberon grandly gestured Kathryn to the room's one and only chair whilst he perched himself on a high stool. Kathryn was immediately reminded of some genial goblin as he smiled down at her, his cheeks bright with excitement.

'First,' Luberon declared, handing across a small, cream-coloured scroll bound by a piece of red cord. 'This is your licence to trade as both apothecary and a spicer.'

Kathryn took the scroll, closed her eyes and heaved a great sigh of relief.

'Simon, I could kiss you!'

The little clerk went puce with embarrassment.

'Oh no, not here.' He blinked. His face became grave, as he bent down and fished amongst the manuscripts on his desk. He held up a small, waxen figure. 'You needn't touch it,' he warned.

Kathryn stared at the black wax, the round domed head, the nail driven through it and the *T* scrawled across the body.

'It's Tenebrae!' she exclaimed. 'His waxen effigy pierced with a nail!'

Luberon threw it to the floor and wiped his fingers on his jerkin.

'One of the market beadles found it yesterday morning, pinned to the cross near the Buttermarket. He only brought it to me after Tenebrae's death became common knowledge.'

'Why should someone do that?' Kathryn asked. 'Take the trouble of creating an effigy, piercing it, then hanging it up in a public place?'

Luberon shuffled on his stool.

'I remembered my father talking about the case of Bolingbroke, the famous London sorcerer who was executed in Saint Paul's churchyard in London. Bolingbroke apparently waged a relentless war on fellow sorcerers. Anyway,' Luberon continued, 'to kill a sorcerer, one must first fashion such an effigy, including the manner in which he is to die, and pin it up in a public place.'

'What it does prove,' Kathryn observed, 'is that whoever killed Tenebrae was desperate and determined enough to do that.'

'It also means that Tenebrae's death was a premeditated act. It was intended that he should die yesterday. But listen.' Luberon got down from his stool. 'I have someone you should meet.'

He scurried out of the chamber. Kathryn kicked the black effigy away with the toe of her boot. She undid the scroll and smiled as she studied the ornate, copperplate writing and the seals at the end, which gave her the right to trade as an apothecary. Kathryn murmured a prayer of thanks. She had struggled for this for over a year, fighting the opposition of the traders, her kinsman Joscelyn, himself a spicer, as well as those who simply envied her good fortune. She stared at the dust, which covered a pile of parchment whilst she made a quick calculation: if she continued to work as a physician both for herself and for the council, the profits from her trade might make life very comfortable. She then recalled Foliot's threat about Colum.

'If Colum went,' she whispered, 'what would be the use?'

'Mistress Swinbrooke?'

Kathryn started as Luberon ushered into the room a squat, sandy-haired man, his long, dirty cloak coated with sawdust. The man shuffled his feet and smiled in embarrassment at Kathryn.

'This is Thawsby,' Luberon explained, 'one of Canterbury's finest craftsmen and furniture makers. He heard about the death of Tenebrae and came, early this morning, to tell me a strange story. Well, go on now, tell Mistress Swinbrooke!'

'What about the Irishman?' Thawsby muttered. 'I thought there'd be an Irishman present. You know, the King's Commissioner?'

Kathryn smiled. 'I'll tell him what you say, Master Thawsby.'

The man closed his eyes. 'A week, no ten days ago, or was it nine days ago?'

'Get on with it!' Luberon hissed.

'Oh yes, eight days ago Master Tenebrae comes into my shop. I knows him and, Mistress, I be afeared of him. So I let him talk to my apprentice, but then he beckons me over in that imperious way he had. "Master Thawsby" he says.' The carpenter opened his eyes and looked at Luberon. 'Yes, that's what he called me, Master Thawsby. "I want you to make me a bed for my nuptials: the largest and broadest you have". He gave me two gold pieces, described what he wanted and then left. Yesterday I becomes concerned, I have his gold but he's got no bed.'

'I told you,' Luberon muttered, 'you can keep the bloody gold!'

Kathryn suddenly thought of Colum and grinned.

'And you should keep your plans for the wedding bed, Master Thawsby. You never know who your next customer might be.'

Luberon stared at her curiously.

'I knows you,' Thawsby said. 'You be physician Swinbrooke's daughter. A good man. Once . . .'

'Yes, yes,' Kathryn intervened, 'but are you sure that Tenebrae asked for a bed for his nuptials?'

'As sure as my wife's got spots on her bottom.'

'And he never came back?' Kathryn asked.

'No. Now he doesn't need a bed, does he?'

Kathryn thanked him and Luberon ushered him out.

'Well,' he breathed, coming back and closing the door behind him. 'What do you make of that, Mistress Kathryn?'

'What would a man like Tenebrae want with a wedding bed?' Kathryn murmured.

'Thawsby forgot to tell you something,' Luberon replied. 'He said his intended wife was not from Canterbury.'

Kathryn immediately recalled the beautiful Louise Condosti.

'I know what you are thinking.' Luberon was almost dancing from foot to foot. 'The lovely, young maid amongst the goldsmiths: the one who's so pure, you'd think butter wouldn't melt in her mouth.'

Kathryn nodded. 'If Tenebrae married, someone like Louise would be his bride. Young, beautiful and rich.'

'But would she have killed him?' Luberon asked.

Kathryn shrugged. 'I doubt if Hetherington would have been pleased at the match, not to mention her betrothed Neverett. I also wonder how that madcap Morel would welcome his master's new bride?'

'Shall we question them?' Luberon asked.

'No. Let me think on it.' Kathryn rose to her feet. 'But, Simon, I need a favour: Mistress Sempler?'

Luberon groaned.

'You have seen the Justices,' he replied. 'Well, within the week, Mathilda Sempler will appear before them. She has confessed to having a grievance against Talbot. She has admitted cursing him, writing an incantation down.' He shrugged. 'As you know, Talbot fell down the stairs and broke his neck.'

'And have you confronted her?'

'Yes, I have!'

'And?'

'Nothing except that simple smile. She will not deny anything.'

'Where is she lodged?' Kathryn asked.

Luberon pointed to the floor. 'In the dungeons below. I'll take you down there.'

Luberon swept out of his office with Kathryn behind him. He took her to the rear of the Guildhall where a bailiff stood guard by a great, iron-studded door. Luberon ordered him to open it and, taking a torch from the wall, led Kathryn down the slimy steps into the fetid gloom. A turnkey, sitting at the bottom of the steps, rose to meet them. A fat, bulbous-faced man who apparently took his job most seriously. He waved his keys, nodded his head pretentiously at Luberon's whispers, then took them along the corridor, warning them to watch the puddles of water. He opened a cell door and ushered them in. Mathilda was sitting on a collection of old rags thrown over some mouldy straw. She looked no different from when Kathryn had seen her last: bright-eyed, her face seamy and dirty, her long, grey hair straggling down to her shoulders. At first, Kathryn thought she had lost her wits. But then Mathilda suddenly cackled and leaned forward, her face garish in the torchlight.

'You are the Swinbrooke girl. I knew your father. I've told you about cures.'

'Yes, you did,' Kathryn replied. 'And that's why I'm here.

Mathilda, the King's Justices have arrived in Canterbury. You are going to be arraigned on charges of murder and witchcraft.'

The old woman cackled again.

'Murder is what murder is,' she said enigmatically. 'Talbot got his just deserts.' She shrugged. 'They can't prove I killed him.'

'You cursed him.'

'If cursing's a crime,' Sempler retorted, 'then every gaol in the kingdom would be full to overflowing.'

'Aren't you frightened?'

'Oh, I am only an old woman. They'll set me free.' She leaned forward and touched Kathryn's face. 'You've got kind eyes, girl. You have come to ask what you can do to help, haven't you?' She glanced over Kathryn's shoulder at Luberon standing behind her. 'And you are the city clerk. Could you ask these hellhounds for some decent bread and a goblet of fresh wine?' She lowered her head and looked under her brows at Luberon. 'If you do,' she whispered, 'I'll never curse you.'

'Don't be mischievious,' Kathryn retorted. 'Mathilda, I will send you in a fresh dress and some food wrapped up in linen cloths.'

'I'll make sure you are made more comfortable,' Luberon added.

'Is there anything else?' Kathryn asked.

'Yes.' Mathilda leaned forward. 'Tell that bitch, Mistress Talbot, that there are many kinds of witches.'

'What do you mean?'

'Just tell her!'

Kathryn made her farewells, left the gaol and walked back through the Guildhall to the front steps.

'She'll hang for definite!' Luberon declared.

'I know,' Kathryn replied. 'But I am going to see Mistress Talbot. Maybe she'll have pity on an old woman and withdraw the charge!'

Luberon shook his head but Kathryn was already hastening

down the steps. She knew where the Talbots lived and carefully rehearsed her words as she made her way through the busy streets and alley-ways. She ignored the cries of the apprentices and their habit of running out from behind the stalls to pluck at her sleeve or catch her by the front of her dress. The sun was now strong and the thoroughfare packed with traders and droves of pilgrims making their way up to the Cathedral. Only once did she have to pause as a dusty-robed friar, chanting his prayers, led a small funeral cortege down to one of the cemeteries. Now and again the boy leading him would stop and ring his bell and the friar would raise his voice to declaim:

> *Remember man that thou art dust*
> *And into dust thou shalt return.*

The mourners staggered behind, most of them the worse for wear after drinking the funeral ales. At last Kathryn reached Talbot's house: a large, three-storeyed mansion with lattice windows and gleaming, red plaster. It stood by itself; the front and side of the house were lined with stalls heaped high with leather goods and supervised by two journeymen and a cluster of apprentices.

'Even in the midst of death trade goes on,' Kathryn murmured.

She approached the huge front door, surmounted by a large wreath in the shape of a cross placed there as a sign of mourning. She knocked loudly; a maid answered and ushered Kathryn into the passageway where the signs of mourning were more apparent. Black cloths hung along the walls and over the polished furniture. In the small parlour where Kathryn was shown, all the pictures and tapestries had been taken down. The room had been converted to a funeral chamber, its bare stone floor cleared of rushes. Purple and black cloths were draped against the wall and, on a small table next to the hearth, two purple candles burnt before an open triptych depicting a suffering Christ.

'You wanted to see me?'

Kathryn started as Isabella Talbot, followed by brother-in-law Robert, came in. Brief introductions were made and Kathryn immediately felt uneasy. Robert looked slack-jawed and wet-eyed but Isabella, dressed in a black head-dress, veil and fashionable gown of red fringed with black, looked formidable; her beautiful face sharp and arrogant, lips pursed in disdain, as if she regarded the world, and everything in it, as well beneath her notice.

'What do you want?' Isabella asked sharply.

Kathryn's heart sank: she would get little pity from Isabella Talbot.

'My name is Kathryn Swinbrooke. I am a physician.'

'We know that,' Robert interrupted languidly.

'I've come to beg,' Kathryn said, her face becoming hot. 'I've been to the Guildhall. I've seen Mathilda Sempler. She's a madcap old woman and, yet, you will go before the Justices and accuse her of witchcraft and murder.'

'That is the truth!' Isabella snapped. 'She didn't pay her rent so my husband turned her out of her cottage. She cursed him in the presence of witnesses at the parish church. She then had the impudence to write a curse and slip it under our door. My husband . . .' Isabella stopped to blink furiously as if fighting back the tears but Kathryn recognised her falseness. 'My husband,' Isabella continued, 'was a wealthy merchant, well liked and loved. Mistress Sempler's attacks troubled his last days and led to his death. The power of witches is well known, Mistress Swinbrooke. Holy Mother Church,' she concluded sanctimoniously, 'teaches how the devil wanders the earth like a ravenous lion seeking whom he may devour. Don't you believe that?'

'Yes and Holy Mother Church teaches charity and justice to all. You said Mistress Sempler accosted your husband at church?'

'Yes!'

'So, this old woman did attend the Mass and take the sacraments?' Kathryn said.

'We have the Church's teaching,' Isabella replied archly, 'that even Satan can appear as an angel of light.'

'How did your husband die?'

'He fell from the top of the stairs.'

'May I see?'

And before Isabella could make a reply, Kathryn had brushed by her and was out in the passageway striding up the stairs. Her sudden action left the Talbots disconcerted. Robert muttered a protest as he hurried behind, but Kathryn climbed the steep stairs and stood at the top, her hand resting on the newel post. Isabella and Robert came up, watching her curiously.

'Yes,' Kathryn declared before they could speak, 'these stairs are long and steep. A fall down them would seriously wound or kill a man.' She looked at Isabella. 'But couldn't he have slipped?'

'Don't be ridiculous!' Isabella retorted. 'He'd been down these stairs a thousand times!'

'Yes, that's my point,' Kathryn said. 'Why on that occasion did he fall so violently?' She was pleased to see the surprise on Isabella's face. 'You have just admitted it,' Kathryn continued. 'He used these stairs constantly. And when I appear before the Justices to speak on Mathilda Sempler's behalf, I will make that very point.'

'Ah!' Isabella smiled spitefully. 'But that's our case. Why should he slip on that occasion, unless he'd been cursed?'

'What was he wearing?' Kathryn asked.

'A normal pair of boots.'

'Where are they?'

Isabella's eyelids fluttered wearily.

'We gave them away as an act of charity.'

'Why was your husband rushing downstairs?'

'We were in our chamber, talking,' Isabella replied. 'I looked through the window: some urchins were trying to steal things from the stalls. Go and ask the apprentices, they will verify that. I hurried out, my husband followed. I heard a scream.' She shrugged. 'The rest you know. Why, Mistress Swinbrooke, what is the problem?'

'I just want to understand,' Kathryn said. 'Here is a man dressed in good, sound boots hastening down his stairs yet he slips. Surely he could have broken his fall? Grabbed the balustrade?'

'Precisely.' Robert leaned forward, scratching his chin. 'But he didn't, Mistress, because he had been cursed. Next time you go to the Guildhall, look at our sworn statement. What we have told you is now a matter of public knowledge.' He glanced over his shoulder at his sister-in-law. 'And so, if you have no further questions, we must ask you to leave.'

Kathryn did so, walking down the stairs, conscious of the Talbots' hard-eyed stare. She let herself out and walked back into the street. For a while she stood staring up at the window then down at the stalls. She jumped as a hand seized her shoulder; turning round, Kathryn stared straight into Colum's grinning face.

'Irishman, don't do that! You are as soft as a cat. What are you doing here?'

'I went to the Guildhall,' Colum replied, linking his arm through hers and moving her gently farther down the street. 'Luberon wasn't there, but a clerk told me that you had been to see him and that you'd left for the Talbots. So here I came. What news?'

'I have my licence to trade.'

Colum gave a shout of pleasure, which drew all eyes to them, especially as he then squeezed Kathryn in a vice-like hug, kissing her passionately on each cheek. Kathryn kicked him gently on the shins.

'Let me go, Irishman!'

Colum released her. 'You are pleased?'

'Yes I am,' she said tartly. 'And I have been thinking about Master Foliot's threat. You have a glib tongue on you, Irishman. You'd make a splendid trader.'

Colum grinned shyly and, before he could tease her any further, Kathryn described what Luberon had said, then her visit to the Talbots. Colum paused and whistled under his breath.

'The Talbots don't bother me. They are powerful and have a case.' He glanced sadly at Kathryn. 'The best you can do is make a plea for compassion. But Tenebrae was planning to marry, eh? I wonder who the poor unfortunate was?'

Kathryn repeated her suspicions about Louise Condosti.

'But we have no proof of that,' Colum declared. 'The intended bride could be anyone in the kingdom.'

'But he ordered the bed recently,' Kathryn insisted. 'Think, Colum. Louise is the kind Tenebrae would prey on: young, lovely, rich and vulnerable.'

'Through blackmail?' Colum asked. 'What could he know about someone so young?'

'That's the mystery,' Kathryn replied. 'But I intend to resolve it.' She glanced down Hethenman Lane. 'Now, let's walk quickly. I can see Rawnose: to listen to his news twice in one day is more than even the good Lord would expect.'

Kathryn's mood was not lightened when she reached her house. Wuf came dancing out of the door, jumping up and down with excitement.

'Lublon's here! Lublon's here!'

'You mean Luberon?' Kathryn asked.

'Yes, the small, fat man,' Wuf answered cheekily.

'I may be small but I am not fat!' Luberon, his cheeks glowing red, came huffing and puffing through the door. 'Thank God I have found you, Mistress, and you Master Murtagh. We are needed at the Kestrel.'

'Why?'

'Fronzac has been killed. Rose this morning fresh as a butterfly he did. Broke his fast and went to look at those fierce hogs.' Luberon plucked at Kathryn's sleeve, almost pushing her down Ottemelle Lane. 'He must have slipped.'

Kathryn remembered the small, dusty-faced clerk.

'Oh God! Poor man!'

'Killed,' Luberon continued. 'The hogs killed him. Heaven save us, Mistress, I know the Lord must call us all, but sometimes he does it in very strange ways.'

'Was it an accident?' Colum asked.

Luberon shrugged. 'I don't know. Foliot's there. He believes there's mischief afoot.'

Luberon didn't bother to ask about Colum's muttered reply, but hastened on, chattering volubly about the danger of hogs. They found the Kestrel strangely quiet: the stable yard was deserted. The taproom was empty except for Hetherington and his party who clustered, white-faced, round a table. Foliot sat enthroned at the top, like an angel come to judgement.

'Mistress Swinbrooke, you are most welcome.'

He ushered them to seats and shouted at a pale-faced tapster to bring some watered wine.

'What happened?' Kathryn asked.

Hetherington took his hands away from his face and stared down the table at her.

'He got up, like the rest of us,' he replied. 'Came downstairs and broke his fast.'

'I was with him,' Neverett declared. 'He said he wanted to take the morning air. I knew where he was going, he always did every morning.'

'And then what?'

Kathryn watched Louise Condosti carefully. She was sitting still as a statue, her lincoln green dress and gold-edged head-dress emphasizing her pallid beauty.

'No one heard anything!' Hetherington snapped. 'Until a servant came rushing in. He'd found the hogs grunting and rushing about, more excited than usual. When he climbed the fence, he couldn't believe his eyes: Fronzac was lying there being gored by the hogs. The tavern master and some of the grooms plucked his corpse out.' Hetherington put his face back into his hands. 'Lord save us!' he groaned. 'His body was an open sore!'

Kathryn stood up. 'One of the servants found him?'

'Yes, why do you ask that?' Brissot snapped.

'Strange,' Kathryn replied. 'Why didn't Fronzac cry out? Scream? Shout for help?' She glanced at Foliot. 'And the corpse?'

'In the outhouse. I'll show you.'

Luberon whispered he would prefer not to, but Kathryn and Colum followed Foliot out, across the small yard they'd entered the previous evening. A pale-faced groom squatted with his back to an outhouse door. He jumped to his feet as they approached and pulled the door open. Foliot paused and glanced at Kathryn.

'I hope you have a strong stomach,' he murmured. 'Mistress, even on battlefields, I have never seen a corpse like this!'

Chapter 6

Kathryn went into the small hut, lit by oil-lamps placed around that dreadful, bloodstained piece of sheeting on the table. Kathryn ignored the foul odour. She glimpsed Fronzac's limbs sprawled out beneath the sheeting: her stomach heaved at the bloody stump where some hog's sharp teeth had bitten deeply into the dead clerk's foot.

'Uncover him!' she whispered. 'And watch those oil-lamps!'

Colum did so and immediately turned away from the torn, gory face of the dead clerk.

'Jesus Misere!' Kathryn breathed.

She drew nearer, remembering what her father had taught her. 'Clear your mind, Kathryn. Don't reflect! The flesh is flesh, it's the spirit that matters.' Kathryn fought hard to follow his advice: lumps of flesh were missing from Fronzac's cheek and the soft part of his neck; his fingers looked as if he had been tortured on a rack whilst one eyeball had been shifted by a sharpened hoof. Colum came back.

'God have mercy!' he whispered. 'The man was a fool, what was he doing so close?'

'Help me turn the body over!' Kathryn ordered. 'Oh, for God's sake, man, come on!'

Colum obeyed. Kathryn carefully examined the back of the corpse. She peered at where the skull had been caved in.

'Woman, what is the matter?' Colum asked.

'Turn him round again!'

Colum obeyed. Kathryn tapped Fronzac's knife still in its sheath.

'Leave it!' she said. 'Let's visit these terrible hogs!'

Luberon was waiting outside, talking to the groom.

'Mistress Swinbrooke,' he said. 'This is the man who found the corpse.'

Kathryn grasped the groom's hand, noting that his pock-marked face was white as snow, his eyes were still watery from retching.

'I fought at Towton, Mistress,' he began, 'in the terrible snow: corpses were piled waist-high yet nothing like that!'

'Tell me what happened.'

Kathryn moved across to where Colum was washing his hands at the pump. She did likewise, then wiped them on the inside of her cloak. The groom stood, scratching his head.

'I'm trying to forget,' he mumbled.

'Please,' Kathryn said. 'You see.' She pointed to the hut. 'That poor man did not die of an accident. He was murdered. Or so I think.'

The groom's face went slack with surprise.

'Please,' Kathryn repeated.

'I came out for some water.' The groom pointed to the hog pen. 'I could hear them grunting, highly excited, sometimes they are like that. It continued so I became curious. I climbed the fence and looked in. The hogs were milling about. I could see the blood on some of their flanks. Then I saw a boot sticking out. I picked up some stones and threw them; the hogs cleared away: that poor bastard's corpse was lying there.'

'How?' Kathryn asked.

'You know, just lying.'

Kathryn took a groat from her purse, pushed it into the man's hand and pointed to a small patch of grass.

'Show me!'

The man shrugged, but obeyed. He went across and lay down on the grass, legs sprawled, face staring up.

'Thank you.' Kathryn helped the groom to his feet. 'What is your name?'

'Catgut.' The man grinned. 'Well, that's what they call me. It's a nickname.'

Kathryn smiled. 'Tell me, Catgut, if you fell into that pen, what would you do?'

'Try and get out.'

Kathryn laughed. 'No, you are a fighting man. You carry a dagger?'

'Of course!' Catgut whispered. 'That man didn't even draw his.'

Kathryn turned to Colum. 'And wouldn't you do the same?'

'I'd fight for my life.'

'And what else?'

Colum pulled a face. 'Scream and yell.' He smiled. 'Of course, no one heard Fronzac cry out!'

'And what else?' she insisted.

Colum closed his eyes.

'Let's say you have lost your dagger,' Kathryn continued. 'You can't reach the fence. You'd roll over, surely, to protect your head and face. Yet most of Fronzac's bruises are to his front except for that terrible blow to the back of his head.'

Followed by the rest, Kathryn walked down the hog pen. She climbed onto the tree stump beside the fence and peered over: the hogs milled around, bristling backs, tufted ears, short, raised tails, narrow, red eyes gleaming with fury. She looked at their strong legs and the small tusks on either side of their jutting mouths.

'Thank God!' she murmured. 'At least Fronzac was spared this terror.'

She gazed around. The hog pen was a broad square of sturdy planks nailed to posts driven into the ground. It contained a trough, feeding bins, but nothing else except churned mud. Kathryn glimpsed a small gate at the far side, a little lower than the actual fence. She got down and walked carefully round the hog pen.

'What are we looking for?' Colum asked.

Kathryn paused and stared back towards the tavern. She could see the casement windows high in the third storey under the red tiled roof. However, once she was round the other side of the pen, the tavern was obscured. She walked down the path to a wicket gate built into the high, bricked wall. She lifted the latch and stared into the alley-way.

'Where does this lead to?'

'Back into the city,' Catgut replied.

Kathryn closed the gate and leaned her back against it.

'Colum, do you have a penny?'

'Of course, I have two. Do you want them?'

'No, Catgut does,' Kathryn said. 'I want you to search,' she told the groom, 'the bushes on either side of the hog pen.'

'What am I looking for?'

'Oh, you'll know when you have found it. A thick stick, a club: it may be smeared with blood and have some of the dead man's hairs still on it.'

Catgut needed no second bidding, but scurried away, crashing about in the bushes. Foliot, who had apparently returned to the tavern whilst she had been examining Fronzac's corpse, came hurrying round the hog pen. He took one look at Kathryn's eyes and pretty, flushed cheeks and grinned.

'It was murder wasn't it?' he asked. He looked to where Catgut was still crashing about amongst the shrubbery.

'Yes, it was murder,' Kathryn said. 'First, Fronzac wasn't stupid: he was born in the countryside. He knew the danger of hogs. He would never climb the fence and sit with his feet dangling over like some child. No, Fronzac came to this side of the hog pen because his murderer asked him to and, when his back was turned, the murderer struck, hitting him on the back of the head with a club or stick. It was easy to do: the hog pen hides any view from the tavern whilst the boundary wall and the alley-way beyond obscures the view of any passerby.'

'That's why Fronzac didn't cry out?'

'Precisely,' Kathryn replied. 'His body was either thrown over the fence or even dragged through the gates. The hogs, maddened by the scent of blood would finish the assassin's task. If Fronzac had slipped, he would have drawn his dagger, screamed for help and certainly tried to clamber out.'

'I've found it!' Catgut cried, dancing out of the bushes, his face scratched by the thorns. He held up a thick blackthorn cudgel. 'This is it!' he shouted, brandishing it in the air and running back to Kathryn.

She examined the club carefully and pointed to the patch of red, matted hair.

'So,' she murmured. 'We have the corpse, we have the weapon and we know how it was done. Only two matters remain. Who and why?' She glanced at Foliot. 'I'd wager a purse of silver that the assassin is now sitting in that taproom.'

Colum, busily handing over the coins to a now happy Catgut, came back to join them, as did Luberon, still pasty-faced, glancing fearfully back at the hog pen.

'You've learnt something today, Simon,' Colum gently teased. 'Stay well away from hogs.'

'I'll remember that,' Luberon said in a choked voice. 'And, believe me, Irishman, it will be a long time before I have any appetite for pork or bacon.'

'Go back, Simon,' Kathryn instructed. 'Tell the rest of the pilgrims to wait for us.'

Luberon hurried off. Kathryn grasped Colum's hand and held it, staring at Foliot. She wanted to remonstrate with him about his threats the previous evening, but before she could speak, Colum did it for her.

'You left us abruptly last night, Master Foliot.' He pushed Kathryn's hand away, his fingers going to the dagger strapped in his belt. The Irishman took a step forward; Foliot did not move, but stood watching him carefully. 'You said that if I failed to unmask Tenebrae's murderer I might be recalled to London.' Colum struggled to keep his violent temper in check. 'Have you marched under a blistering sun or tried to sleep in the freezing snow? I have. I have been hunted on land and tossed about on the high seas. I do not like to be threatened.'

Foliot stepped back, pushing his cloak over his shoulder, his hand going to the hilt of his sword.

'And now you threaten me, Irishman?'

'Stop it!' Kathryn came between them, her back to Colum.

'What's the matter, Mistress?' Foliot taunted. 'Protecting your Irishman?'

Colum moved angrily, but Kathryn pressed herself against him.

'Don't be stupid,' she whispered. 'My Irishman's no idle boaster. He'd take your head.'

Foliot blinked and glanced away. 'And you would like that, Mistress?'

Kathryn caught the humour in his voice. 'Now you are being stupid.' She stepped away from Colum.

'I am sorry I threatened you.' Foliot held both his hands out in a gesture of peace. He glanced quickly round the small garden as if wary of eavesdroppers. 'You know the Queen,' he whispered hoarsely. 'I'll tell both of you this, just the once. Tenebrae held some terrible secret, about what I don't know. But believe me, Irishman, if I go back to London empty-handed; everyone involved in this business, and I mean everyone, will feel the Queen's anger, including myself.'

Colum relaxed. 'In which case, let's make sure you don't!'

They walked back to the tavern where Luberon and the pilgrims were waiting. The clerk must have told the pilgrims what Kathryn had discovered. Hetherington looked openly worried; Greene anxiously plucked at a loose thread. Dauncey whispered with Brissot whilst Neverett and the beautiful Louise sat, hands nervously clasped. Kathryn put the bloodstained, blackthorn cudgel down on the table.

'Master Fronzac was murdered.' She quickly described how she had reached that conclusion.

The pilgrims listened stony-faced.

'It must be one of us,' Hetherington spoke up.

'Yes,' Kathryn replied. 'Logic dictates that.'

'But why?' Neverett asked. 'Why should someone kill poor Fronzac? He was an able, industrious clerk.'

'Did he have any enemies?' Colum asked.

Neverett grimaced. 'Who hasn't, Irishman? Rivals, personal dislikes but certainly not the rancour and malice which leads to murder. He was no threat to anyone.'

Hetherington interrupted. 'Except Tenebrae's killer?'

'Yes,' Kathryn declared. 'And I'll speak honestly. Tenebrae was killed by someone in this room. Fronzac, God knows how, learnt something. He was murdered because of that knowledge.' She paused, her words hung like a noose above the pilgrims.

'Did Fronzac say anything?' Colum asked. 'Last night, or this morning, anything untoward, was he silent or withdrawn?'

'Far from it.' Brissot, his neat moustache almost stiff with excitement, shifted his bottom on the little stool, his fingers tapping the table. 'He was happy: more than I have seen him for some time. After you left last night, he and I stayed down here. We shared a bowl of wine. We talked about Tenebrae's death, then the affairs of our Guild in London. Fronzac said he was hoping to move, buy a grander house near the Bishop of Ely's inn just north of Holborn, one with a garden and carp pond.'

'Did he explain the source of his newly found wealth?' Kathryn asked.

'Oh,' Brissot replied, quivering with self-importance. 'We didn't touch on that. But, there again, he was a bachelor and he must have money stowed away.'

'Yes, he did,' Hetherington added quickly. 'He lodges his money with me. Master Fronzac was not a wealthy man, but he had enough for the comforts of life.'

'And did he speak to anyone else?' Kathryn asked.

The pilgrims stared back at her. Brissot turned and pointed to Louise.

'Mistress Condosti, he spoke to you. Remember? After we left the taproom we returned to our chambers. You came out, you were looking for a fresh candle. He took you aside, whispering.'

The young woman, so pale-faced Kathryn thought she was about to swoon, opened her pretty lips to reply then, bowing her head, began to sob.

'What did he talk about?'

Louise just shook her head and dabbed at her eyes.

'Don't bully her!' Neverett shouted, pushing back his stool.

'You will sit down,' Colum said firmly.

'I will question Mistress Louise by herself,' Kathryn intervened. 'So that can wait. Did anyone else speak to Fronzac?'

Again a wall of silence.

'He came down here this morning to break his fast,' Hetherington said in exasperation. 'The usual courtesies were exchanged.'

'Then what happened?' Kathryn asked. 'I mean precisely?'

'He said he must go out into the garden.'

'Must?' Kathryn queried. 'Are you sure he said that, Sir Raymond?'

'Yes, yes, he did.'

'And where were the rest of you?'

A babble of answers broke out, which Kathryn stilled by questioning each of them individually. Hetherington and Greene said they were in their chambers. Neverett claimed he had walked into the city to view the market trade. His betrothed, Condosti, still dabbing at her eyes, simpered that she had stayed in her chamber. Dauncey and Brissot also declared they had gone for an early walk in the city to see the stalls and booths along Queningate.

'So none of you went into the garden?' Kathryn asked.

She turned and called over the master taverner who was leaning against the door of the kitchen. He bustled across, his cheery face now solemn.

'You heard what was said?' Kathryn asked. 'Master . . . ?'

'Byward,' the taverner replied. 'Anselm Byward.'

'Is it true?' Kathryn asked.

Byward nodded. 'Catgut has already told me his tale.' He wiped his hands on his apron. 'I've questioned everyone: scullions and grooms. According to them, only the man who was killed went out into the garden. What is more, I have just learnt from my wife that the gate behind the hog pen was not unbarred until after the corpse was found. To put it bluntly, Mistress, if anyone entered that garden, they must have climbed the wall.'

Kathryn thanked the taverner, who went back to his listening-post to watch this drama unfold and speculate whether it would be good or bad for business.

'What are you implying by all this questioning?' Greene snapped.

'I am implying nothing,' Kathryn retorted. 'Fronzac left the taproom saying he must go out to the garden: that means it wasn't just a pleasant morning's jaunt. I suspect he was going to meet his murderer.'

'But no one followed him out,' Brissot piped up.

'The murderer could have still climbed the wall.' Hetherington snorted. 'Which means, Mistress,' he tapped his broad belly, 'I am not the assassin. I find it difficult to climb stairs, never mind vaulting high walls.'

'Who told you it was high?' Foliot interrupted.

'I have been out there,' Raymond blustered, his face going puce with anger. 'And I am becoming tired of you, sire. Where were you this morning?'

All eyes turned to the Queen's emissary and Kathryn quietly cursed her own stupidity. No one was above suspicion. Foliot was a glib courtier, talking in hushed tones about great secrets, but could he be the assassin? He had visited Tenebrae the morning the magus had died. He also knew where the pilgrims were staying. Foliot seemed to read her thoughts, and he smiled slyly.

'I can vouch for my movements,' he declared. 'If you go to the tavern where I am staying, you'll find I have more witnesses than people attending Mass on a Sunday.'

Luberon leaned over. 'Mistress,' he whispered. 'This questioning is leading us nowhere.'

Kathryn agreed and got to her feet. 'Louise.' She smiled at the dark-eyed beauty leaning on her betrothed's shoulder. 'I need to speak to you alone.'

Louise looked up, eyelids fluttering. She darted a glance at Hetherington, who rubbed his face in his hands.

'No one need accompany you,' Kathryn insisted. 'Except Sir Raymond.'

Hetherington touched the young woman's shoulder.

'Is that what you want?'

Condosti nodded.

'What about me?' Richard Neverett exclaimed, pushing back his stool, his face anxious and puzzled.

'You will stay here!' Hetherington boomed, getting to his feet.

The Guildmaster led both Kathryn and Louise up the stairs on to the first gallery and into his opulently furnished chamber. Its walls had been painted a brilliant white, the stone floors covered in rugs and brightly embroidered tapestries hung against the wall. The four-poster bed was of polished oak and decorated with green curtains fringed with gold. There was a table, a few stools, a chest and two high-backed chairs. Hetherington closed the door, waved both Kathryn and Louise to these and pulled up a stool to sit opposite them.

Kathryn wiped her slightly sweating palms on the front of her dress as she tried to curb the trickle of excitement in her stomach, the same feeling she had when diagnosing a patient and discovering the cause of some mysterious ailment. For the first time, the wall of silence these powerful goldsmiths had built around them was about to be breached.

'Mistress Condosti,' Kathryn began bluntly. 'I have questions to ask about your relationship with Tenebrae.'

Condosti's lower lip began to quiver.

'Please,' Kathryn whispered. 'I do not wish to bully or harass you. Did Master Tenebrae propose or hope to marry you?'

Condosti's eyes flew open. Kathryn caught a look of subtle cunning and knew she had missed the mark.

'Mistress Swinbrooke!' Condosti smiled. 'Marry Tenebrae!' She threw her head back and pealed with laughter.

Kathryn glanced at Hetherington: he, too, was smiling, visibly relaxed. Think first, speak later! Kathryn ruefully recollected. Through her work with patients, Kathryn had become quite skilled in questioning but, listening to Condosti's laughter, she realised she had a great deal more to learn.

'How could you say such a thing, Mistress Swinbrooke?' Hetherington brayed.

Kathryn shrugged. 'I am just clearing obstacles from the path: first things first!' Kathryn decided to grasp the nettle. 'What I do know is that Tenebrae was blackmailing you, wasn't he, Louise?'

Condosti stopped smiling.

'Oh, not over money,' Kathryn continued. 'Or political allegiances, or giving aid and comfort to the King's enemies. Something more, how can I say, personal?'

Louise nodded, her eyes brimming with tears.

'I'll answer for her,' Hetherington spoke up. 'As you know, Mistress Condosti is my ward. I have given her every comfort and luxury, as much freedom as she wishes. Perhaps a little more than I should have done.' He leaned over and patted Louise affectionately on her hand. 'Two years ago, Mistress Swinbrooke, the King and the House of York were overthrown, Margaret of Anjou and the Lancastrian faction entered London. In that army came many adventurers, including an impoverished French nobleman, Charles de Preau. Now de Preau was handsome, charming, dashing and gallant.' Hetherington paused and licked his lips. 'London was in turmoil. The Lancastrians were desperate for money. I and the other goldsmiths were summoned to innumerable banquets and festivities. The real purpose was to obtain monies at the lowest rate of interest possible. Louise accompanied me to a splendid supper held at Sheen Palace: feasting, dancing, revelry, even the fountains ran with wine. She met de Preau: clever in speech, most sensitive in his dealings and learned in all the subtleties of romance.' Hetherington glanced at Kathryn. 'Must I spell it out, Mistress Swinbrooke? Louise was really no more than a child. She gave her heart to de Preau; he seduced her.'

Louise sat, back rigid, hands in her lap, staring down at the floor.

'Louise is no longer *virgo intacta,* as the malicious gossips would say, she is used goods.'

'Such an occurrence,' Kathryn replied briskly, 'is not a matter for condemnation.' She smiled at Louise. 'The heart can be a wayward guide yet how could Tenebrae come to know something like that?'

'Because,' Louise replied flatly, 'I became pregnant, Mistress Swinbrooke. Two months later the Lancastrian forces left London, de Preau was killed at Barnet. I miscarried, the child within me died. Tenebrae must have heard about it.'

'Who tended to you?' Kathryn asked.

'Brissot,' Hetherington replied.

'Ah!' Kathryn leaned back in her chair.

'I am not saying,' Hetherington asserted, 'that Brissot was the source of the information. Others knew.'

'Does your betrothed, Neverett?' Kathryn asked.

'I think he does,' Louise replied shyly. 'One day I will have to tell him.' She rubbed her mouth and Kathryn saw she was trembling. 'But, to be fair to Brissot, as Sir Raymond said, others also learnt about it.'

'Who?' Kathryn asked.

'Members of the Guild,' Hetherington replied. 'Greene and Dauncey undoubtedly suspected.'

Kathryn studied Louise carefully. She showed no relief, her hands were still trembling as she played with the gold tassels of the cord round her waist. Kathryn leaned over and squeezed her ice-cold fingers.

'There was more, wasn't there? Tell me,' Kathryn insisted. 'Why should a lovely young woman like you be closeted with a creature like Tenebrae?'

'Because I was in love!' Louise cried. 'Mistress Kathryn, have you ever been in love? I loved Charles de Preau with all my heart and mind. Every time I came to Canterbury I visited Tenebrae to discover how our relationship would end.'

Kathryn caught the steel in the young woman's voice and sensed the emotions bubbling hotly within her.

'Oh, Tenebrae was good,' Louise continued. 'He'd play those damned cards: it was he who prophesied the danger, showing me the two of swords. After Charles was killed I was convinced.' She dried the tears from her cheeks. 'Last autumn I came back here with Sir Raymond and the rest: this time Tenebrae was different. He told me my future and claimed that, unless I did exactly what he told me, my shame would be announced to the world and its wife.'

'What did he do?' Kathryn asked.

'He said I was beautiful,' Louise said. She glanced from under lowered eyelids at Hetherington. 'I should have told you this, but . . .' She paused for a while. 'He made me strip,' Louise whispered. 'He made me strip in front of him, then walk around the room.'

Hetherington sprang to his feet, his face mottled with fury.

'May he be damned in hell!' he roared and crouched down beside Louise. 'Why didn't you tell me? Did he touch you?'

Louise shook her head. 'No: that's all he made me do. He promised me silence and that he would conjure up the future and make all things well. I did it because I felt trapped. It was like a dream. Afterwards I would pinch myself.' She shrugged prettily. 'And that was all.'

'Did you hate him?' Kathryn asked. 'Mistress Condosti, did you hate Tenebrae?'

'Sometimes, yes. Sometimes myself.' Her voice rose. 'Sometimes life, Charles: everything had become a tangled mess.'

'And Master Fronzac?' Kathryn asked.

Louise's eyes held hers: they had lost their dove-like softness and showed the steel beneath the velvet.

'He knew!' she spat out.

'What do you mean?' Hetherington exclaimed.

'Fronzac knew,' Louise declared. 'Oh, to you, Sir Raymond, he was the industrious clerk. Yet, did you ever stop and study him carefully? Those watery eyes, that slack mouth? I used to catch him watching me, sometimes sitting next to me, wetting those cracked lips whilst he pressed his leg against mine, only to apologise volubly.'

'What did Fronzac say to you last night?' Kathryn insisted.

Louise laughed abruptly. 'Do you know, when I heard Tenebrae had been murdered, I was pleased. Suddenly everything seemed calm: Tenebrae was dead, no more threats, no more walking round that terrible room. However, last night, when I came upstairs the nightmare returned. Fronzac pulled me aside. He asked after me. Was I not pleased that the magus had been killed?

I just looked at him then he said: *"One day, Mistress Condosti, if you know what is good for you, you must walk round my chamber as you did for Tenebrae."*

'I was horrified. I fled.' She laughed sharply. 'Now Fronzac is killed. I wonder if I have some curse upon me. Should I really be betrothed to Master Neverett?' She rose quickly to her feet, drying her eyes and pinching her cheeks to bring the colour back. 'I have told you what I know, Mistress Swinbrooke, before God I have.' She glared down at Sir Raymond. 'Perhaps it's best if others did the same.'

And, without a second glance, she walked out of the chamber, slamming the door behind her.

Hetherington sat ashen-faced.

'The Church,' he murmured hoarsely, 'orders us not to dabble or have anything to do with the likes of Tenebrae.' He glanced up at Kathryn. 'Believe me, now I see the wisdom of it.'

'What did your ward mean?' Kathryn asked. 'That others should tell me the truth?'

She paused at a knock on the door and Colum entered. Kathryn gestured at the seat beside her.

'What is happening?' Colum asked. 'Mistress Condosti came running down and straight out into the garden.'

'I'm learning some truths,' Kathryn replied. 'And Sir Raymond, I think, will tell us some more, though not for the moment. Sir Raymond, may we use this chamber?'

The goldsmith nodded. 'I need some wine,' he said, rising to his feet. 'I'll be in the taproom with the rest.' He walked out of the chamber like a beaten man.

Kathryn and Colum followed him. Foliot and Luberon were waiting in the gallery outside, the little clerk's eyes sharp with curiosity, Foliot more calm. Kathryn assured them all was well, but asked them to stay with the pilgrims, explaining how she and Colum wished to interrogate each one individually.

'I should be present,' Foliot declared.

'No,' Colum retorted. 'You have made it obvious that the responsibility for this matter is mine. I must insist that you leave matters be, at least for a while.'

Foliot pulled a face and followed Luberon down the stairs. Colum turned to Kathryn. 'What is the matter?'

'Master Fronzac had the grimoire,' Kathryn replied. 'He was murdered because of its secrets.'

Chapter 7

Back inside the chamber, Kathryn gave Colum a pithy description of what had happened. He stood by the window, listening to her carefully.

'So,' he concluded. 'Master Tenebrae's intended bride, perhaps, does not concern us, but the whereabouts of the grimoire does.' He shook his head. 'Yet it doesn't make sense. How could Fronzac murder Tenebrae and take the Book of Shadows? Bogbean assured us the clerk left the house that day like everyone else. And, after his departure, the magus was visited by others, not to mention his own servant Morel. So,' Colum slumped down on a chair, 'where do we go from here?'

Kathryn wove her fingers together and stared at the expensive cloth hangings round the bed. Thomasina would like those, she thought, thick and heavy: difficult to clean but sturdy enough against the passage of time.

'Kathryn?' Colum insisted.

She smiled apologetically. 'What we have done, oh dark-browed Irishman, is at least breach the wall these goldsmiths have built round themselves. Condosti had a great deal to hide and implied her companions also did. Perhaps it's best if we saw them one at a time: we should start with Master Brissot.'

Colum went down to the taproom and returned with the rotund little physician, who came in brushing his neat moustache, blinking nervously as Kathryn invited him to sit.

'Master Brissot,' Kathryn began smilingly. 'How much did Tenebrae pay you?'

The physician nearly fell off his stool. 'What are you saying?' he stuttered. 'How dare you?'

'Shut up! You know full well what I mean. You are a London physician, hired specially by the goldsmith's guild for the care of their fraternity. You scurry around from house to house, you attend their functions and your sharp little eyes miss nothing. You were Tenebrae's spy and told him about Condosti's condition. Didn't you ever suspect what such a hideous creature might do with such information?'

Brissot stared back.

'I'm giving you the opportunity,' Kathryn said conversationally, 'to tell me the truth. If you lie, or we later discover you have lied, Master Murtagh here has powerful friends at court. He will make it his business to proclaim to the city what you are and what you do.' Kathryn remembered Condosti's fear and hurt, and pulled her chair closer. 'And how would you prosper then, Master Brissot? I am a physician; we hold a secret trust to keep our mouths shut about what we know.'

Surprisingly, Brissot began to cry, the tears rolling down his red cheeks, his shoulders shaking uncontrollably. Kathryn stared in amazement and steeled herself against the sight of this pompous, little man blubbering like a child. At last he stopped, swallowed noisily and lifted his face. Kathryn flinched at the hatred blazing in his eyes.

'Do you think I liked it?' he asked slowly. 'I, Charles Brissot, a student of the Sorbonne, Padua and Marseilles, in the hands of a man like Tenebrae?' He shook his head. 'I deserve everything you have said but, Mistress Kathryn,' he leaned forward and tapped the side of his head, 'up here the demons and ghosts dwell, in the dirty recesses of our minds. Don't you have any? Well, I do.' He dried his cheeks with the back of his hand. 'You had to know Tenebrae to understand his wickedness. He was subtle and wily. Like some fat spider, he would invite you into his web, and once you were caught, he held you fast.'

'And how did he trap you?' Colum asked.

Brissot turned to him. 'You put me there,' he retorted, 'or men like you. Yes, I am physician to the goldsmiths of London but, in the summer of 1471, I was hired as a physician for King Henry VI when he was imprisoned in the Tower of London.' Brissot glimpsed the surprise on Colum's face. 'Yes, yes, the saintly Henry VI of the House of Lancaster: a man more devoted to his prayers than the crown. You know the story? After the Yorkist victories at Barnet and Tewkesbury, Henry VI, a prisoner in the Tower, mysteriously died there.' He stared at a point above their heads. 'He didn't die. The poor, saintly man was murdered, his head being dashed against the wall, his emaciated body pierced with daggers.' Brissot paused and drew in his breath. 'I had to tend to him, dress the corpse, before it was moved downriver to Chertsey for burial. So, what does it look like to you, Irishman? To be the physician who attended his corpse, who knows the truth but has to keep his mouth firmly shut.'

'It's true,' Colum whispered. 'The rumours abound about how Henry died. He perished the same night the King and his brothers held a banquet at the Tower. The official proclamation says he died of natural causes.'

'Tenebrae taunted me with that,' Brissot broke in. He glared at Kathryn. 'For God's sake, Mistress!' He laughed abruptly. 'Here I am, walking the streets of Canterbury, paying homage to Becket, an archbishop killed by a king. Yet look at me: a physician who knows a saintly king was murdered. Tenebrae offered to voice that to the world.' He shrugged. 'So I had to tell him everything I knew. All the tittle-tattle of the Guild; who said what to whom: the scurrilous petty scandals that plague all our lives.' He spread his hands. 'Yes, I told him about Louise Condosti and other matters.'

'Then tell us about these matters,' Kathryn replied. She held her hand up. 'I give you my word. We only want to trap Tenebrae's killer.'

Brissot smiled. 'Aye, I'll tell you: the same I told that bastard of a magus. How Hetherington was furious at Tenebrae's knowledge about Condosti. How that same goldsmith lent purses of silver to the Lancastrian faction. How Thomas Greene likes young boys, with angelic faces and full, white buttocks.'

'And Neverett?' Kathryn asked.

'Oh, he's fairly guiltless. A young man not yet steeped in sin.'

'And what about Dauncey?' Colum asked.

'Why not ask her yourself,' Brissot replied. 'Talk to the good widow. Ask about her constant hunt for a husband.'

'She is comely enough,' Kathryn tactfully intervened. 'And she is very wealthy.'

'Aye,' Brissot replied. 'Her last husband owned ships. In reality he was nothing more than a common pirate. Most of his wealth was ill-gotten.'

'But she is still wealthy?'

Brissot got to his feet. 'I have told you enough.' He leaned down, his face only a few inches away from Kathryn's. 'I didn't kill the magus,' he rasped, 'but I wish to God I had!' And spinning on his heel, he walked out of the chamber.

'Well, well, well!' Colum stretched. 'Nothing is what it appears to be and, in this case, all that glitters is not gold.'

Kathryn rose and slipped behind him, pulling gently on his hair.

'No time for Chaucer now, Colum,' she murmured. 'There is no need to speculate. I wager every one of them had good cause to hate and kill Tenebrae.'

'Where's the grimoire?' Colum asked.

'We'll deal with that in a minute,' Kathryn said. 'First, we must have words with the good Widow Dauncey.'

Colum went down to the taproom and returned with Dionysia, one hand resting gracefully on his arm, the other clutching her cane.

Kathryn studied the widow's thin, lined face carefully. Her eyes were bright enough, but her skin had a sallow, unhealthy complexion: as she sat down in the chair, Kathryn saw how she gripped her stomach as if in pain before daintily arranging the folds of her dark blue gown, then the coif round her greying hair. She sat demurely with her hands in her lap, her bright eyes watchful.

'Mistress Swinbrooke,' she began softly, 'you are to be congratulated. Never did a woman upset so many people in so short a time.'

'It was not my intention,' Kathryn retorted. 'But, as Master Brissot says, we have, in our souls, dark recesses where we do not want others to pry. And yet?' Kathryn shrugged. 'A man like Tenebrae had the gift for penetrating such shadows.'

'He was very good,' Dauncey replied. 'Sharp and mysterious. A shrewd mind and a quick eye. He knew the importance of ritual and appearances. He persuaded us to think he had powers, perhaps he did not.'

'How long have you been a widow?' Kathryn asked.

Dauncey smiled, trying to hide her yellowing, cracked teeth.

'Four years. My husband died at sea and, before you ask, Mistress Swinbrooke, he was my third husband.'

'And do you have children?'

'Oh, no.' Dauncey's laugh was forced, her fingers gripped the side of her stomach.

'You are in pain, Mistress Dauncey?'

'Why?' the widow snapped. 'What did fat, little Brissot tell you?'

'He told us nothing we did not know: that Tenebrae was a proficient blackmailer. So, what power did he have over you?'

Dauncey stared bleakly. 'I don't . . .' she stammered. 'I can't . . .'

'You are ill with some sickness,' Kathryn interrupted.

She studied the woman carefully: beneath the thick powder and rouge, Kathryn glimpsed small sores at the corner of the widow's mouth. Dauncey was about to shake her head then she flailed her hands in a pathetic gesture and glanced away, blinking furiously to hide her tears.

'I envy Mistress Condosti,' she whispered. 'Her beautiful face and body, warm and ripe like an apple to be plucked. I wish, Mistress Swinbrooke, that I could be plucked.' She stared down at a costly ring on her index finger. 'People look at me and think, "Ah, there goes Widow Dauncey, well respected, wealthy and a pillar of the Church". Yet I toss in my bed at night like a cork in a stream!'

'But you have suitors?' Colum asked.

Dauncey laughed nervously. 'Oh, yes, and how the tongues clack: old Widow Dauncey pursuing some young men. I would like to marry.'

'Then why don't you?'

'Because, Mistress Swinbrooke,' Dauncey leaned forward, her face mottled with anger, 'I have a disease. The undying legacy of my last husband.' She sat back. 'He could sleep with everything and probably did, be it a dog or some raddled whore in one of the many ports he visited.' She pointed to the sores on her mouth. 'It grows within me. Who will marry me, Mistress Swinbrooke, a rotting, old woman? That's what Tenebrae knew.'

'Did Brissot tell him?' Kathryn asked.

'No.' Dauncey shook her head. 'I have my own physician though much good it will do me now.' The tears welled in her eyes.

'Please don't publish it abroad, Mistress Swinbrooke, but I was about to marry.' She smiled. 'I hid it from the rest.' Her voice shook. 'Only this morning I visited Procklehurst in Iron Bar Lane. I was looking for a marriage ring for my betrothed. Go there yourself,' she offered, seeing Kathryn's surprise. 'That was one secret Tenebrae didn't know. Fronzac the clerk, he'd offered to marry me. It wasn't a passionate romance of the heart but . . .' She plucked at a loose thread on her gown.

'You were going to marry Fronzac?' Kathryn asked.

'Yes.' Dauncey held out her hand. 'He gave me that ring two days ago.'

Kathryn saw the band of gold.

'Who do you think killed him?' Kathryn asked.

Dauncey shook her head. 'If I knew that, Mistress Swinbrooke, I'd carry out vengeance myself.' She rose to her feet. 'But I tell you this. Sir Raymond Hetherington and his party have a great deal to hide, as does Master Foliot.' She smiled down at Kathryn. 'Oh, yes, he may not recognise me, but I remember Theobald Foliot very well.'

'Don't speak in riddles!' Colum snapped.

'He's the Queen's creature,' Dauncey retorted. 'So, tell me, Master Murtagh, you who have served the Yorkist cause so well: Elizabeth Woodville, before her marriage to her king, was the widow of John Woodville an ardent Lancastrian?'

Colum nodded.

'Foliot,' Dauncey concluded, 'was one of John Woodville's principal henchmen. So, God knows what he has to hide!' She then swept out of the room.

Colum put his face in his hands. 'We've hunted murderers, Kathryn,' he said slowly, 'people who have killed with no apparent motive, but here everybody has one!' He straightened in his chair. 'One thing does concern me. Tenebrae was a magus, a collector of information, a blackmailer.' The Irishman pointed at

Kathryn. 'You, Mistress, whether you like it or not, are now a leading citizen of this city. I wonder if he knew anything about you or me?'

Kathryn pulled a face and clapped Colum heartily on the shoulder.

'If he did, I couldn't give a fig. But the riddle of his death continues. It would be easy to finish our accounts, draw a line and claim Tenebrae was killed by Fronzac who was later murdered himself, yet that pail doesn't hold water. Tenebrae was alive when Fronzac left his house and we still don't have the grimoire.'

'Let us say, for sake of argument, that Fronzac did not kill Tenebrae. Then how did Fronzac know about Louise Condosti? Such an intimate matter, so personal?'

'I don't know,' Kathryn answered. 'Tenebrae could have told him or, perhaps, Fronzac was another of his spies.' She breathed in deeply. 'But I understand what you say: the first and only time Fronzac taunted Louise was after Tenebrae's death.'

'Perhaps Fronzac was always Tenebrae's spy,' Colum wondered, 'and the magus shared tidbits of information with him. Once Tenebrae was dead, Fronzac thought he would use such juicy morsels for his own pleasure.'

'Perhaps,' Kathryn replied, moving towards the door. 'Let's have Master Foliot here and search Fronzac's chamber for the grimoire.'

Colum hurried down and returned, Foliot behind, grinning like a cat.

'You disturbed a wasp's nest down there, Mistress Swinbrooke! When I return to London, I must recommend you to His Majesty's justice. You have a sharp eye.'

'Not sharp enough.' Kathryn briefly described the conclusions she had reached. 'Fronzac may have killed Tenebrae, stolen that grimoire and then used its secrets against Mistress Condosti.' She paused. 'Fronzac must have thought he would become the new blackmailer, but this morning received short shrift for his pains.'

'In which case,' Colum pulled a key from his pouch, 'Fronzac should have the grimoire and I have the key to his chamber.'

He led them along the gallery and stopped before a chamber door which he unlocked. Inside, the room was tidy, curtains pulled neatly around the small, four-poster bed. Clothes hung from a peg driven into the wall beside a small window. The dead man's possessions were neatly piled on a chair: a soiled, canvas shirt, a belt and a battered wallet that only contained a few coins. Kathryn lifted the lid of the chest at the foot of the bed. Inside were more of Fronzac's possessions, but she could see nothing of the grimoire. She took out a small scroll then stood up, easing the cramp in the small of her back. She stared round the small, whitewashed chamber.

'It truly is the Book of Shadows,' she murmured. 'Where could it be?'

'Fronzac may have hidden it,' Colum replied.

And, whilst he and Foliot pulled back the curtains of the bed, rummaging under the eiderdown and bolsters, Kathryn went and sat in the small window seat and undid the scroll. She carefully read the letter from Dionysia Dauncey. She felt a little guilty: it was a love note. It mentioned, in passing, the death of Tenebrae, but then went on to describe their nuptials, planned to take place on the Friday after the feast of Corpus Christi in Saint Mary-Le-Bow. Kathryn was surprised at the passion in the letter. Dionysia described her longing and her determination to buy a ring from Procklehurst, a name Kathryn recognised as one of the leading goldsmiths in Canterbury. She noticed the date at the end of the letter was the previous day. She rolled the letter up and handed it to Foliot who was staring curiously down at her.

'It's only a love letter,' Kathryn explained. 'Probably written late yesterday. A few sentences.' She smiled and glanced away. 'A woman like Dionysia would find it hard to express her feelings under the watchful eyes of the pilgrims.'

Colum joined them.

'Nothing!' he exclaimed. 'If Fronzac had the grimoire, then it's gone.'

'Someone could have stolen it,' Foliot observed. 'After he was killed.' He waved his hand in a gesture of despair. 'On second thought they couldn't have. The landlord said there was only one key to the chamber and he took it from Fronzac's corpse.'

'And no one else had asked for it?' Kathryn said.

Foliot shook his head. 'They wouldn't would they? The finger of suspicion would point directly at them. All we have for our trouble is another mysterious murder and a love letter from Widow Dauncey.' He tapped this against his cheek. 'We had better give it back to her.'

They returned downstairs. The pilgrims had gone out into the garden. Kathryn and Colum left Foliot to make their farewells and return Dauncey's letter whilst they went into Queningate and up, through a narrow alley-way, into the High Street.

'Does it make any sense to you?' Colum asked. He pulled Kathryn to the doorway of a tavern to accomodate a motley collection of pilgrims who were pushing a cripple in a handcart towards the cathedral gates.

'At the moment, no.' She looked across the busy High Street: the stalls and booths were doing a roaring trade as droves of pilgrims left the cathedral to wander the market-place and take refreshment. Suddenly she felt hot and tired.

'Let's sit for a while.'

She tugged at Colum's sleeve and led him into a low-ceilinged taproom. A scullion brought them jugs of cool, musty ale and a platter to share, containing bread, cheese and a small bowl of onions chopped and covered with parsley. Colum drew his knife and neatly cut portions for Kathryn.

'Be of good cheer.' He smiled across at Kathryn. 'If we don't resolve this mystery, Master Foliot certainly will.'

Kathryn slowly chewed on the soft, fresh cheese.

'What happens,' she asked, picking up another piece, 'if Master

Foliot is part of the mystery? He visited Tenebrae the morning before he died. He is strong and able enough to climb that tavern wall, attack poor Fronzac and throw his corpse into the hog pen.'

'But that is true of all of them,' Colum interrupted. 'They all saw Tenebrae the day he died, whilst any one of them had the strength to drag a senseless Fronzac into the hog pen.' Colum drained his tankard. 'What more can we do?'

Kathryn sighed. 'At the moment nothing. There's no order here, Colum. No logic to events. Tenebrae was alive when all the pilgrims left. Nobody went up to that chamber afterwards whilst Fronzac's death is just as mysterious. However, we've learnt something. First, all those pilgrims have secrets they prefer to keep hidden. Secondly, once they were in Tenebrae's net, they hated the magus. Thirdly, that grimoire, the Book of Shadows, somehow or other, fell into Fronzac's hands. Finally, therefore, whoever killed Fronzac now has it.'

Colum rose to his feet, dusting the crumbs from his jerkin.

'Well, physician, I have to leave you.' He stared round. 'By the way, where did Luberon go?'

'Probably still back at the tavern.'

Colum nodded and they went back to the High Street. Now distracted by the problems waiting for him at Kingsmead, he absent-mindedly kissed Kathryn on the cheek and wandered off, muttering under his breath.

Kathryn watched him go, then made her way along Burghgate. She paused at the corner of Iron Bar Lane, where she caught sight of the goldsmith's sign with Procklehurst's name neatly painted across it. She went to the open door of the shop, carefully slipping by the stalls set out in front and manned by the apprentices. The room inside was dark and cool: the windows were shuttered and candles had been lit along the long, oval table that dominated the room. As in any goldsmith's, nothing was on display. The gold geegaws were being sold on the outside stalls under the watchful eyes of the apprentices whilst, inside, the goldsmith would do business and only bring out those precious items customers required.

Kathryn picked up a small bell on the table and rang it. Master Procklehurst came bustling out of the chamber. His head was bald as a pigeon's egg, his fat, jowled face well oiled and bristling. His gimlet eyes quickly assessed Kathryn's worth. He rubbed his hands.

'You wish to do business, Mistress? Deposit monies? Perhaps see some bauble that's not on display outside?'

A faint smile played round his lips as if he judged Kathryn worthy of such welcome. She was tempted to say she had a purse of gold coins which she hoped to bank just to see if that smile broadened.

'Well?' Procklehurst stepped closer, twitching his expensive, ermine-lined robe around his shoulders.

'I am Kathryn Swinbrooke, physician.'

Procklehurst's smile faded. 'Oh, the one hired by the Council?'

'No, Master Procklehurst, the one who works with the King's Commissioner, Master Colum Murtagh.'

Procklehurst's smile returned. 'Of course,' he purred. 'How can I help?'

'You know Dionysia Dauncey, a widow and goldsmith from London?'

'Oh, yes.' The merchant's smile widened. 'She was here this morning.'

'Master Procklehurst,' Kathryn snapped. 'I am sure you are busy but so am I.'

'Mistress Dauncey came here,' Procklehurst continued quickly, 'to purchase a gold ring.'

'And she definitely bought one?'

'Oh, yes, then I placed it in a coffer for safe keeping. She seemed very excited, talking about her forthcoming marriage.'

'Thank you.' Kathryn turned and left the shop as abruptly as she had entered.

She walked down Iron Bar Lane. A legless beggar, pushing himself along the rutted track in a cart, came trundling after her, whining for alms.

'Lost my legs!' he cried, his dusty face twisting into a grimace. 'Lost my legs to the Moors in Outremer!'

Kathryn gave him a coin and watched as he pushed his way back to his begging post on the corner of an alley-way. She wiped the sweat from her brow with the cuff of her gown and walked on across Saint George's Street into Lamberts Lane near White Friars. She still felt agitated and cursed her own bad temper.

'Think sweet thoughts,' she murmured to herself. 'Otherwise, Swinbrooke, you'll become a harridan, a veritable fishmonger's wife.'

There was a small green near the Carmelite monastery, which ran down to a duck pond where children played noisily in the shadows, splashing each other with water whilst the ducks and swans swam serenely around them. Kathryn sat down on a bench in the shade of a large sycamore tree. She leaned back and watched the children play. Her father used to bring her here as a child, pointing out the various plants and explaining how some of the birds who came there flew hundreds of miles from strange, exotic countries beyond the Middle Sea.

'Don't ask me why,' he would sigh. 'That's one of God's mysteries.'

Kathryn narrowed her eyes and smiled. 'Why is it that children love water?'

She fought against the nostalgia that threatened to overwhelm her. Images of childhood tantalised her mind: the days were always warm and sun-filled, her father studying a plant whilst she played around him. When she grew older, he would take her to the great mystery plays at All Saints, or Blackfriars north of the city. Kathryn realised how faint such memories had become. Her marriage to Alexander Wyville, the drunken, wife-beating apothecary, lay like a great, black wall across her life cutting it into two.

Now Alexander had gone, following the armies of Lancaster, and Kathryn did not know whether he was alive or dead. Her father had died and she had drifted, supported and comforted by Thomasina until Colum had come swaggering into her life. And what would happen if he left? Kathryn closed her eyes. No wonder she was bad tempered, she thought; brooding always produced black humours.

In the shade of a sycamore tree Kathryn forced herself to reflect on the mystery of Tenebrae. If she solved that, all would be well. She closed her mind to the sounds around her as she recalled her visit to the dead magus's house; those broad, sweeping stairs leading to his room, the doors that could only be opened from the inside. The chamber itself, dark and macabre. Each pilgrim had left by the back door, gone along the small gallery and down the stairs where Bogbean stood on guard. The windows were all shuttered, Kathryn knew. No one could get into that room without Tenebrae's permission. So how, in God's name, did he die? Each pilgrim goes in, each pilgrim goes out. Tenebrae is alive. Morel spoke to him just after noon but then goes back up to the chamber and finds his master dead, shot by a crossbow bolt. And who would carry such a bulky weapon? And Tenebrae? Why didn't he shout out? Fight back? Try to escape? Kathryn opened her eyes and shook her head.

'Impossible!' she muttered. She breathed in deeply and thought about Fronzac's battered corpse being thrown into the hog pen. 'Think,' Kathryn muttered. 'Fronzac goes out to the hog pen. He walks to the far side away from the tavern where no one can see him. Then what happens?' She paused to collect her thoughts. The rest of the pilgrims were either in the tavern or out in the city. None of them were seen to leave the tavern and go into the garden whilst the gate in the back wall had been bolted. The landlord claimed it wasn't opened until after Fronzac's corpse had been discovered. So the killer must have climbed the wall. And who was able to do that? Foliot? Brissot? Neverett? Or even Greene or Sir Raymond? But was the gate locked?

'Kathryn?'

She looked. Father Cuthbert stood in front of her, a basket slipped over his arm.

'Kathryn?' He drew closer. 'What on earth are you doing here?'

'Oh.' She laughed. 'Just resting. And I could ask the same of you, Father.'

The priest nodded towards the walls of the Carmelite monastery.

'I have just been to see the Prior. He kindly agreed that the sheets and blankets of the hospital be washed in his laundry.' He tapped the basket. 'In return I always take him some herbs and potions for the infirmary.' Father Cuthbert sat down beside Kathryn. 'He died, you know.' His gentle eyes studied Kathryn. 'The man you visited. John Paul, I won't use the diabolical name he gave himself. He died with his face towards God: I am sure the good Lord will have compassion.'

Kathryn remembered the man lying against the white sheets: his determination to find and destroy the Book of Shadows. She looked at Father Cuthbert.

'Do you believe in black magic, Father? That men like Tenebrae can call up Satan?'

The old priest put the basket down and pointed to the children playing in the shallows.

'I believe in the good Lord,' he said. 'Sunshine, children laughing and playing. That's the way the world should be, Kathryn. But to answer your question bluntly, men like Tenebrae, through the evil of their lives, can attract dark forces. In their arrogance, witches and warlocks believe they can use such powers, but the sad truth is, it is they who are being used. Now . . .' He got to his feet and stretched his hand out at Kathryn. 'You should stop brooding, Kathryn. Go back to Ottemelle Lane, talk to Thomasina, listen to

Agnes's chatter or play with Wuf. Lose yourself in the ordinary, calm current of your life.'

Kathryn smiled and got to her feet. 'If only everything was so simple, Father.'

'Oh, but it is,' the priest replied, his smile faded. 'It is we who twist and make things difficult.'

Chapter 8

As Kathryn made her way back to Ottemelle Lane, ruefully reflecting on Father Cuthbert's advice, Morel stood in a derelict corner of the graveyard of Saint Mary Bredman church. He stared down at the freshly turned heap of soil that marked the grave of Master Tenebrae. Morel was puzzled. The clerk Luberon had arranged for his master's corpse to be buried here without bell, book or candle. No Masses had been sung. No prayers recited. Instead, the city bailiffs had brought the cheap, wooden coffin into the graveyard, dug a hole, lowered it and left Morel to cover it up. The magus's servant scratched his head. His master would agree with that; he never did like the power of the priests and, in Morel's experience, had never darkened the door of a church. But what would happen now? Should he come back at night and sacrifice a black cock above the grave, allowing its fresh blood to soak the soil? Would his master need such power? Morel shuffled his feet impatiently. He stood, eyes closed, and then he recalled Mistress Swinbrooke. He opened his eyes and smiled. His master had told him what to do.

* * *

Kathryn's hopes of a quiet afternoon to prepare a meal to celebrate the granting of her licence were rudely dashed as soon as
she entered the house. Rawnose was sitting in the kitchen. The
beggar's mutilated face glistened with sweat as he delivered his
news to Thomasina, Agnes and a wide-eyed Wuf.

'All the Justices are there,' he declared as Kathryn came into
the kitchen. 'Bedecked in their scarlet and ermine, armed with
sword and gibbet they will execute the King's justice.'

'I know.' Kathryn winked at Thomasina.

'Ah!' Rawnose's dirty finger pointed to the ceiling. 'What you
don't know, Mistress, is that the Justices of Oyer and Terminer
are already sitting in the castle hall. The jury has been assembled
and our friend Mathilda Sempler is due to appear,' Rawnose
paused for effect, 'at the fourth hour after mid-day!'

'So soon,' Kathryn whispered.

'Aye, the Justices are in a hurry.' Rawnose licked chapped lips
and glanced over his shoulder at the buttery. 'A list of man's wickedness faces them. Arson, robbery, theft, the stealing of a pyx
from a church, a knifing in the Swindlestock tavern, the violation
of virgins, the despoiling of widows . . .'

'Rawnose, enough!' Kathryn interrupted. 'Thomasina, bring
our guest a jug of ale and some oatcakes.' She smiled at the beggar
who gathered his rags about him as regally as any judge would his
robes. 'You've been down to the castle?'

'Oh yes, the Commission of Oyer and Terminer has already
begun.'

'What does it mean?' Agnes spoke up. 'Oyer and . . . ?'

Kathryn gratefully accepted the jug of ale Thomasina brought
her.

'The King's Justice of Assize is in Canterbury,' Kathryn explained. 'They will hear the life and death cases and determine
judgement. However, before a case can reach them, one of the
judges holds a court called Oyer and Terminer, a lawyer's term
meaning to listen and terminate. What will happen to poor Ma-

thilda is that she will be put before a jury. If they believe there's a case to answer, the Justice will commit her to trial at the Assizes, probably some time next week.' Kathryn put the ale down and rubbed her face.

'You should rest.' Thomasina came over and patted her shoulder. 'You look tired.'

Kathryn got to her feet.

'No, Thomasina, someone has to speak for old Mathilda.' She glanced at the hour candle. 'It's already between three and four. I'll go down to the castle.'

'I'll come with you,' Thomasina offered.

'And me!' Wuf spoke up, dancing from foot to foot. He plucked the wooden sword from his belt. 'I'll free Mathilda!'

Agnes also offered to go whilst Rawnose quickly drained his tankard.

Kathryn glanced at them all. 'In which case,' she declared, 'You'd all better come!'

Thomasina bustled around, busily locking cupboards and doors. Kathryn splashed some water on her face and they left, going along Ottemelle Lane into Wistraet. They hurried through the late afternoon crowds, avoiding the carts driven by tired-eyed peasants who, having sold their produce, were making their way towards Worthinggate and the villages beyond.

A small crowd had gathered outside the castle gate and was being held back by guards. An officer recognised Kathryn, as she had been there the previous year to investigate the death of the Constable. They were allowed to pass without hindrance into the yard where a tipstaff took them up into the Great Hall. This had been dramatically changed since their last visit. The grimy walls had been freshly whitewashed, the great beams painted black whilst precious cloths covered the walls, displaying both the arms of England as well as the personal insignia of each judge. Royal serjeants wearing their blue, red and gold tabards had cordoned off the lower end of the hall for spectators. Farther up Kathryn glimpsed the King's Justice sitting on the dais behind a long table, clerks, scriveners and advisers on either side of him. Just below the dais, to the right, sat a jury of Canterbury burgesses and, facing the dais, a long bar had been slung from wall to wall. Here the prisoners would stand whilst the Justice's clerk read out the list of charges. The Justice would then ask questions and the jury would reply. For a while Kathryn and the rest who, thanks to Thomasina's bulk, had pushed themselves to the front, heard this litany of human misery. An arsonist who had set fire to a hayloft. A whore who had assaulted a customer with a knife. A thief who had stolen a pyx from a city church. Kathryn's heart sank: the Justice was not inclined to mercy. His questions were blunt and quick and the harassed jury given little time to reflect.

'Come on! Come on!' The Justice banged his small hammer on the table. 'What reply do you make? What reply do you make?'

Time and again the leader of the jury would stand, shuffling his feet nervously.

'There's a case to answer,' he'd squeak.

'You what?' The Justice cupped his ear. 'Speak up, man!'

'There's a case to answer, my Lord.'

'Of course, there bloody well is!' the Justice roared. 'Take the prisoner away!'

At last Mathilda Sempler's name was called. The old woman came shuffling in through a side door, wrists and ankles secured by manacles. She moved so slowly the Justice snapped his fingers impatiently. The turnkeys gave her a shove so she almost collided with the bar. The scribe read the charges out, finishing with the proclamation: '*And those who have business before His Grace's Justice of Oyer and Terminer draw close!*' In all the other cases this had been a mere formality, but now Isabella Talbot, resting on the arm of brother-in-law Robert, swept out of the side door. She was still dressed completely in black, a lace veil hiding her features. She looked every inch the grieving widow.

'Now!' Thomasina hissed.

Kathryn waved over a royal serjeant and whispered in his ear. The man released the rope and allowed Kathryn and Thomasina up before the bar. The Talbots were standing to Mathilda's left as far away as possible, not only to distance themselves from the accused, but because the old woman stank sourly. Kathryn schooled her features as she gently tapped Mathilda on the shoulder. The accused turned, bright-eyed, and smiled up at her.

'What's this? What's this?'

The Justice, who had been expecting a brief hearing, banged his hammer on the table and glared at Kathryn. Hard-eyed under thick, white eyebrows, he looked as sour as vinegar; by the twist to his lips, Kathryn knew she would find little compassion here.

'What's this? What's this?' The Justice drummed bony fingers on the table.

On either side of him, the clerks just bowed their heads, intent on their scribbling.

'You should not touch the prisoner!' the Justice bellowed, eyebrows raised in shocked disbelief.

Kathryn gazed coolly back, and the justice lost some of his composure.

'It's against all usage! It's against all usage!' He tapped his hammer against the table. 'Mathilda Sempler, you are accused of witchcraft and murder!' He turned to Isabella. 'What evidence do you proffer?'

The old judge forced a smile as Isabella raised her black-edged veil and began to recite tearfully the same tale she had told Kathryn.

'So.' The justice steepled his fingers. 'Your husband threw this woman out of a cottage because she failed to pay her rent. She cursed him in the church porch and later sent the same curse to him on a scrap of parchment?'

'Yes, my lord.' Isabella's voice quivered with grief. She then turned and shot a malicious glance at Kathryn.

'And on the morning your husband died,' the judge continued, 'he was hurrying downstairs because thieves, and some of those same buggers may well be appearing before me soon, were filching goods from his stalls?'

'Yes, Your Honour. I espied them from our bed chamber window. My husband ran out.'

The old judge leaned back, his hands resting on the quilted arms of his chair. 'Clear as anything to me.' He glared at Mathilda. 'Did you curse him?'

The old woman nodded.

'Did you send that curse?'

'Yes,' Mathilda whispered.

The justice looked at Kathryn.

'And what have you to say about all this?'

'Mathilda Sempler,' Kathryn declared, 'is an old woman. She dabbles in herbs and potions.'

The justice leaned over to listen to one of his clerks whisper in his ear. He straightened up, indicating with his hand for Kathryn to be quiet.

'I can see she's old. And I know she dabbles in potions but that doesn't stop her being a murderer, does it, Mistress Swinbrooke?' He leaned forward. 'I understand you are a city physician and also dabble in potions?'

'I am a healer,' Kathryn retorted.

'Yes, and one who is wasting my time.'

'I am also wasting my own time,' Kathryn replied, 'coming here to seek justice. My lord, I, too, am involved in royal business. I work with Colum Murtagh, King's Commissioner in Canterbury; we are presently trying to discover the murderer of the magus Tenebrae.'

The justice's jaw fell slack. He leaned back to listen to his clerk whisper once again. This time he forced a smile.

'Like a silver plate on a coffin lid,' Thomasina whispered.

'Mistress Kathryn,' the justice said. 'I did not mean to give offence.'

'You have!' Robert Talbot exclaimed.

'Shut up!' the justice snapped. 'Mistress Swinbrooke, you were going to say?'

'Your Honour,' Kathryn began, conscious of the whispering from the jury and the crowd at the back of the hall. 'I thank you for your kindness. All I am saying,' she glanced down at Mathilda leaning against the bar, 'is that Mistress Sempler may have cursed Sir Peter, and with good cause, but in law there is no proof that her curse caused Talbot's death.'

The justice, now wary of Kathryn, nodded solemnly.

'True, true.'

'Your Honour,' Robert Talbot now spoke up. 'Mistress Swinbrooke cannot prove that the witch's curse did not kill my brother.'

Again the justice nodded and glanced expectantly at the jury.

'What say ye?'

The leading jury man, however, was sharp enough to sense what was happening. He shuffled to his feet.

'My lord, we believe there is a case to answer, but . . .'

Kathryn's heart leapt.

'If Mistress Swinbrooke can produce evidence to clarify the situation then . . .'

He flapped his hands and sat down as the justice glared at him, then Mathilda.

'You are to be returned to the city gaol,' he intoned, 'until Mistress Swinbrooke can produce further evidence.' He glanced pityingly at Kathryn. 'But, if not, you Mathilda Sempler, will go on trial.' The justice's face hardened. 'If you are found guilty, then the penalty will be terrible. You will be sentenced to hang in a cage above a burning fire until dead.'

Kathryn quickly grasped Mathilda Sempler, otherwise she would have slumped to the floor.

'Take the prisoner down!' the justice roared.

Two turnkeys seized the old woman by the arms and hustled

her out. Kathryn walked down the hall even as the clerk began to read out the next indictment.

'Kathryn, you did well,' Thomasina whispered, plucking at her sleeve.

Kathryn glanced despairingly at her. 'Did I, Thomasina? What further evidence is there?'

They rejoined Rawnose and the rest at the back of the hall, then went out into the fading sunlight.

'Can you help Mathilda?' the beggar man asked anxiously.

Kathryn leaned against one of the buttresses of the castle wall and stared across at the goose wandering around, its long neck straining, looking for morsels to eat. Two boys ran by carrying a pitcher of water from the butts which stood near the warren. Somewhere in the stables a young girl was singing a lullabye. Kathryn closed her eyes. It was difficult to imagine the ordinary things of life going by after such a terrible sentence had been pronounced. She looked down at Agnes and Wuf.

'You should not have come.'

'Will they do that?' Agnes asked, white-faced.

'Aye, the cruel bastards will,' Thomasina interrupted. 'It's what is called a double punishment. The burning is for murder and the slow death in a cage for witchcraft. I saw it happen myself once, when old John Tiptoft, Earl of Worcester, crushed some rebels and found a warlock in their company.' She grasped Kathryn's hand. 'Come on, Mistress.'

They walked back into Wistraet. Kathryn stopped and looked round.

'Where did the Talbots go?'

'Oh,' Thomasina scoffed. 'They left by the side door.' She narrowed her eyes. 'Are you thinking the same as me, Kathryn? She acts the grieving widow a little too perfectly.' Thomasina's double chins quivered. 'I should know. I've been one three times.'

Kathryn glanced at Rawnose. 'Well, my herald of Canterbury.

You may not have a nose, but you have the finest ears in the city! Have you heard any scandal?'

The beggar man's face broke into a grin. 'No, but I will. I know where the Talbots live, their servants are bound to frequent the nearest tavern.'

Kathryn slipped a coin into the calloused hand. She grasped Rawnose by the shoulder and kissed him on his unshaven, chapped cheek. For once the garrulous Rawnose did not know what to say. He touched his face and looked down at the coin as if wondering which was the more precious.

'Find out,' Kathryn insisted. She glanced down at Wuf. 'And then come to our supper party tonight.'

Little Wuf's face lit with pleasure. 'Party, what for?'

'I didn't tell you,' Kathryn said. 'I have obtained my licence to trade as a spicer and an apothecary.'

She couldn't say anything else. Thomasina gripped her in a vice-like hug whilst Agnes and Wuf danced round, clapping their hands. Even Rawnose indulged in a strange, shuffling dance before making his farewells.

'To dig for some juicy tidbits!'

Kathryn and the rest walked back home. Thomasina now diverted everyone's attention by exclaiming how Agnes would look after the kitchen whilst she would look after the shop. On the corner of Ottemelle Lane they met Helga, the rotund wife of Torquil the carpenter. She was in a great state of agitation, using her apron to wipe the sweat from her face.

'Thank the Lord!' she exclaimed, grasping Kathryn's arm. 'And may all the saints in the kingdom of God bless your way. May they bless you in your sleeping and in your waking.'

'Thank you, Helga.' Kathryn was used to the religious hysteria of Torquil's wife. She had not decided whether the woman was out of her wits or really a saint.

'It's Torquil,' Helga explained. 'The Lord is calling him.'

By now Wuf and Agnes were giggling. Even the garrulous Thomasina was staring, pop-eyed, at Helga's strange antics.

'He's dying!' Helga screeched.

'Nonsense!' Kathryn replied. 'He came to me last week with the stomach gripes and the flux in his bowels. I gave him a mixture of angelica and camomile. He was to drink sweet water mixed with honey and a faint trace of wax. He should be in his workshop.'

'Well, come with me!' Helga exclaimed, grasping Kathryn's wrist.

The physician told Thomasina to take Agnes and Wuf back to the house whilst she followed Helga through the narrow alleyways to Torquil's house in Hawks Lane. The downstairs shop was all shuttered up and, in the garden behind, Helga explained, the apprentices were looking after the children. Kathryn followed the carpenter's wife up the wooden stairs, speechless at how many crucifixes hung on the walls whilst every niche held a small statue of some patron saint. In the bed chamber above the solar she found Torquil resting against the bolsters, crisp, white, linen sheets tucked up under his chin.

'The Angel of Death is very close!' Helga solemnly intoned. 'I can hear the beat of his wings.' She threw herself down beside the bed. 'Lord have mercy! Christ have mercy! Lord have mercy! Our Lady, Saint Joseph who was a carpenter . . .'

Whilst Helga finished her verbal assault on the Heavenly Court, Kathryn pulled back the bed-sheets. She felt Torquil's skin, hot and dry, and noticed how his cheeks were sucked in, the lips bloodless. She slipped her hand beneath his night-shirt.

'He's burning,' she exclaimed.

Torquil's head moved and his eyelids fluttered. He opened them and looked up at Kathryn.

'Help me please!' he whispered. 'Is it the plague?'

Kathryn forced a smile. 'Nonsense!'

'I took the medicine,' Torquil whimpered. 'Mistress Swinbrooke, I feel worse.'

Kathryn glared at Helga, whose voice was now rising as she reached Saint Malachai and began her tirade to all the great Celtic saints.

'Helga!' she snapped. 'Remember, the good Lord helps those who help themselves. Stand up and come here!'

The carpenter's wife obediently trotted round the bed.

'What has Torquil eaten or drunk?'

'Nothing,' Helga wailed, hands clasped to her ample bosom. 'Nothing.' Her eyes became more calculating. 'Nothing except your medicine, Mistress.'

Kathryn sat down on the bed, clasping Torquil's hand, which felt as dry as a withered leaf. 'If anything,' she murmured, 'what I gave him should have brought his slight fever down, not increased it.'

Kathryn stared round the cosy bed chamber. Small oil-lamps had been lit and placed in chafing dishes. Helga had sprinkled dried herbs over these to make the air sweet; nevertheless, Kathryn caught the stench of sickness.

'Are you well, Helga? You and your children?'

'Oh, yes, never in better health.'

Kathryn stroked the side of Torquil's face. 'I will brew something. A very special potion.' She recalled her father's instructions about an herbal remedy used by the great Gaddesdon: a concoction of moss juice mixed with the scrapings of dried milk.

'I don't think he should take anything else from you,' Helga snapped. 'I put my trust in prayer.'

'Then why did you come for me?' Kathryn asked. 'Helga, I agree. Torquil is very ill, but I don't know the source. It can't be infected meat or drink. It's not the sweating sickness. Look,' Kathryn got to her feet. 'I will come back later this evening and bring some medicines.'

Kathryn glimpsed the obstinate look on Helga's face and had no illusions what would happen to the potions. They would be tossed on to a midden heap. Torquil would grow worse and possibly die. Kathryn hitched her cloak round her shoulders. She knelt down and pressed Torquil's hand and glared at Helga who was already threatening to go back to her litany.

'There's nothing you can do,' Helga shouted. 'I put my trust in God and the waters of Jordan!'

Kathryn stood up. 'Your prayers to God I understand, but what in heaven's name are the waters of Jordan?' She walked round the foot of the bed. 'Helga, what have you been giving Torquil?'

The carpenter's wife rubbed her hands on her apron, her eyes fluttered nervously.

'Helga!' Kathryn demanded. 'I want to see this water of Jordan!'

Helga breathed in noisily, then sank to her knees, stretched under Torquil's bed and brought out a small, wooden flask sealed at the top by a dirty rag and a piece of twine. The flask had a crudely painted red cross daubed on it. Helga handed this over and Kathryn groaned. The wood was splintered. She sniffed at the rag; it smelt rank and sour.

'I bought it,' Helga wailed. 'There was a man near the Buttermarket, dark-skinned he was, he had been to Outremer.' Helga's hand came up dramatically and she pointed at the flask. 'It comes from a puddle in which both John the Baptist and the good Lord himself stood near the Jordan.'

Kathryn undid the cord. She threw down the piece of rotten rag and sniffed the flask.

'Oh, Lord! It smells like a midden.'

Kathryn went to the window, opened it and, ignoring Helga's screeches of disappointment, tossed the flask out. Kathryn listened, with some satisfaction, as it smashed into the garden below. Torquil's grubby-faced children came running up.

'Don't touch that!' Kathryn shouted, quickly regretting her hot temper.

Due to the angle of the window, she could hear, but not see the children. Kathryn pointed to one of the apprentices.

'Keep them well away.'

She turned and marched back to Helga, sitting on the edge of the bed, face in her hands.

'Helga, look at me.' Kathryn picked up the piece of dirty rag and sat beside her. 'Listen, Helga,' she began quietly. 'You did not know it, but you have been poisoning your husband. If that water's from Jordan then I am the daughter of the Great Cham! More people die,' Kathryn continued, 'from ignorance and filthy water than anything else. God knows where that came from! Helga, you are a tidy woman, your house is neat and clean.' She pushed the rag under Helga's nose. 'Smell that! Why must you think that dirt and sanctity go hand in hand?'

Helga sniffed the rag and pulled a face. 'But it cost me tuppence!'

On the bed behind her Torquil groaned in his fevered sleep.

'Will he die?' Helga asked. 'Oh, sweet Lord, Holy Mary, Saint Joseph, Saint Gabriel, Saint Raphael!'

Kathryn grasped Helga's hand. 'Promise me,' she insisted. 'Promise me you'll never buy anything like that again.'

Helga nodded and solemnly raised her right hand. 'I swear by the straw in Christ's manger.'

'Enough of that!' Kathryn replied briskly, getting to her feet. 'Helga, you have your own well? So, I want you to give Torquil as much water from that as possible, served in a cup that has been carefully scoured. Mix a little honey with it. I'll send Agnes round with the potion. You are to give him it at least four times a day and nothing else. Promise me!'

Helga nodded. Kathryn went back to the window.

'I am sorry,' she said. 'I shouldn't have tossed the flask.' Kathryn craned her neck. 'I can't see it from here.' Kathryn's heart skipped a beat as she recalled Mathilda Sempler and Isabella Talbot standing before the justice in the castle hall. 'Of course,' Kathryn breathed. She put a hand to her lips then remembered the filthy rag she had been handling. 'Come on, Helga!' she declared. 'Torquil will live, if you do exactly what I say. Now, let's go down to the garden and clear up the mess I've made. Afterwards, we'll both scrub our hands and look after Torquil properly. In a week, God willing, he'll be busy in his workshop.'

A rather subdued but happy Helga took her downstairs. Kathryn went into the small garden, picked up the remains of the wooden flask and carefully buried them in the rubbish heap. She stood looking up at the window to Torquil's chamber and noticed how the wall sloped outwards: someone standing close to the wall couldn't be seen from above. Kathryn then went inside. She washed her hands in some rose-water, promised Helga she would send the medicine as quickly as possible and, lost in her own thoughts, walked back to Ottemelle Lane.

Thomasina was already preparing what she triumphantly called a great feast: thick pea soup, oysters stewed in ale, venison steaks cooked in red wine, roast pork with carroway and strawberries in a rich butter sauce. She, Agnes and Wuf were buzzing like bees round the kitchen, full of the sweet, savoury smells of cooking. Kathryn absent-mindedly greeted them. She placed the licence she had obtained at the Guildhall in her writing-office and, once again, carefully washed her hands. She took a small, stoppered jar, made up the medicine for Torquil and, for peace and quiet, allowed Agnes and Wuf to take it to Helga. Once they had gone, hopping through the front door, shouting and singing, Kathryn sat in her writing-office staring at the wall. She made a mental note to ask Simon Luberon to have the pedlars and quacks who preyed on the likes of Helga banned from the city. She leaned back against the high chair.

'What happened to Torquil,' she murmured to herself, 'applies to everything. There was no mystery in his illness. Once Helga talked of Jordan's water, the mystery was solved.'

Kathryn drummed her fingers on the desk. She found it difficult to concentrate. She felt tired and uncomfortable, the sweat
trickling down between her shoulder blades. She seized a piece of
parchment, pen and quill and drew a plan of Tenebrae's house.
The staircase, the chamber guarded by two doors, which could
only be opened from the inside. The stairs and back door which
could not be opened from the outside and was watched by a garrulous Bogbean. Kathryn studied her rough diagram.

'It's impossible,' she observed. 'Each of Sir Raymond's companions met the magus and left. Tenebrae was still alive after
they'd gone. We know that from Morel. Ergo,' she scratched her
cheek, 'what was the solution? Was Tenebrae killed before any of
the pilgrims arrived? Did someone take his place? But who?
Foliot?' Kathryn chewed her lip. Did he disguise himself in the
magus's costume? Kathryn shook her head. Impossible. Kathryn
concluded: some time or other, Foliot would have to leave and
either Morel or Bogbean would have seen him. Kathryn tapped
the quill against the desk, quietly cursing as the ink splattered her
fingers. She seized the scrap of parchment and wrote Morel's
name on it. Was the dead Tenebrae's servant more cunning than
he appeared? He claimed to have spoken to his master after the
pilgrims had left. But was he telling the truth? It would be so simple to tap on his master's door and, when it was open, fire the
crossbow and leave. But why should Morel do that? He had nothing to gain, or had he? Kathryn vowed to have fresh words with
Morel. She then turned to Fronzac's death.

'How,' she whispered, 'had someone been able to enter that
garden, strike him on the back of the head and toss his body
amongst the hogs?'

She heard the door open.

'Helga said thank you!'

Kathryn turned to where Agnes stood in the doorway. She
smiled at her and Wuf who was jigging up and down beside her.

'Are there any other messages?' the lad cried. 'We are good at delivering messages, aren't we Agnes?'

Kathryn was about to shake her head, but then she remembered Fronzac's death and the back gate to the tavern.

'Yes, there is,' she exclaimed. 'Agnes, I want you to go to the landlord of the Kestrel. Ask him one question. Who opened the gate in the wall of the back of his tavern?'

'Is that all?' Agnes asked.

'Yes.' Kathryn smiled.

'Can I go?' Wuf cried.

'Yes, and tell Thomasina to give you some marchpane. Go straight there,' Kathryn called as both Agnes and Wuf ran down the passageway into the kitchen. 'I want you back within the hour!'

For a while Kathryn sat listening to Agnes and Wuf pestering Thomasina in the kitchen. They came hurrying back, shouting their farewells, the doors slamming behind them. Kathryn seized another piece of parchment and from memory sketched the outlines of the Talbot house and the stalls around. However, she found her eyes growing heavy so she cleared the desk and went upstairs to her own bed chamber where she stripped and carefully washed herself, using the sponge and a piece of precious soap from Castille. Thomasina had already filled the water in the lavarium bowl and left a fresh pitcher in the corner. Afterwards Kathryn felt better. She slipped on a linen shift and sat on the bed listening to the sounds from the kitchen below as Thomasina thundered around. Despite her tiredness Kathryn would have liked to have helped but she knew Thomasina: the best cook in Canterbury her father had called her, but highly dangerous if disturbed in the mysteries of the kitchen. Kathryn lay down on the bed and stared up at the rafters. Colum would soon be home whilst Rawnose, who could smell a good meal from ten leagues away, would be back with whatever gossip he could garner. Kathryn recalled the waspish face of the judge.

'He won't be sentencing old Mathilda,' Kathryn murmured to herself.

She was certain she had found a flaw in Isabella Talbot's argument, but to prove it, she needed Colum's help. And as for Tenebrae, the Book of Shadows and Fronzac's murder? Kathryn's eyes grew heavy. There was something she had heard today, but she was so tired that she had forgotten: still wondering about this, Kathryn drifted into a deep sleep.

Chapter 9

Colum's return from Kingsmead woke Kathryn. She dressed and went down to the kitchen to help Thomasina, busily shooing the ravenous Irishman away from the cooking pots.

'Keep your hands to yourself!' Thomasina snapped.

Colum winked at Kathryn. 'It's so delicious,' he teased. 'I'm spoilt for choice. The food or you, Thomasina, eh?'

Kathryn kissed him on each cheek.

'You need a shave, Irishman.' She sniffed. 'Horse and leather.'

'Aye!' Colum sat down on a stool. 'More horses have arrived from the King's stables. Some were put down in the river meadows, others will have to stay in the stables.' He looked sharply at Kathryn. 'The manor's nearly finished. Strong roofs, the flooring sound and the walls are plastered. After May Day they will be whitewashed.' He looked around the kitchen. 'And then, I suppose, I'll have to move out?'

'Aye and there'll be more food for us,' Thomasina interrupted.

'You don't have to go,' Kathryn said.

Colum stared at her coolly, and Kathryn turned back to Thomasina.

'Has Agnes returned?'

As if in answer to her question, there was a rattling at the door and both the maid and Wuf came hurrying down the passageway.

'We delivered the message,' Wuf cried. 'And the man said this . . .'

'Hush!' Agnes seized Wuf's arm. 'The landlord was nice. He gave us some sweetmeats.'

'And my question?' Kathryn asked.

Agnes closed her eyes and scratched her head. 'Well, he said the gate was locked at night, but now you ask, neither he nor any one in the tavern can remember opening it this morning.' Agnes stared expectantly at her mistress. 'That's all he said.'

Kathryn thanked them and they ran off to the buttery to wash their hands and faces before helping Thomasina. Kathryn filled a tankard with ale for Colum.

'What was all that about?' the Irishman asked.

'Just one little piece in the puzzle,' Kathryn replied. 'Remember, Fronzac went down to the hog pen. I wondered who had opened the gates at the back of the tavern. Now I have my answer, probably Fronzac himself. He went there to meet someone, well away from the prying eyes of the other pilgrims.'

Colum sipped from the tankard.

'Now who could it be, eh?' Kathryn asked. 'Strong enough to strike an able-bodied man and toss his body into a hog pen?'

'And the whereabouts of his fellow pilgrims?' Colum asked.

'At the tavern or in the city. However, one of them went to the back of that tavern and knocked on the gate: Fronzac opened it and let his murderer in.'

'If it was one of the pilgrims,' Colum intervened. 'Master Foliot is a mystery in himself.'

'Aye.' Kathryn played with a crumb lying on the table. 'And there's Tenebrae's servant, Morel. We only have his word that his master was alive when all the pilgrims left. True,' she continued, 'I can't see any motive for Morel murdering his master, but he was alone with Tenebrae after all the pilgrims left.'

Colum put the tankard down. 'So, we should question him again. Morel might have had one motive.' He paused. 'Tenebrae left no will. Now, Master Luberon could advise us on this. If there are no relatives, Morel could, as the only surviving relict, lay a claim in the court of chancery that he has a legitimate claim to Tenebrae's property and monies.'

'Could he do that?' Kathryn asked.

Colum grinned. 'It's wonderful what a good lawyer can achieve.' He drained his tankard, muttered about changing for supper and went up to his chamber.

Agnes and Wuf returned. The kitchen became so noisy Kathryn went back to her writing-office. For a while she reflected on what Colum had said, but steeled herself against any quick, easy conclusions. Morel was an easy victim. He had no powerful patrons and it would be as unfair to lay allegations against him as it had been for Isabella Talbot to accuse poor Mathilda Sempler. Kathryn sighed and returned to the kitchen.

Colum washed, shaved and changed, came down and everyone became involved in the frenetic business of laying the table and ensuring all went well. Rawnose returned, chattering like a squirrel till Thomasina roared at him to shut up. At last dinner was served. Colum toasted Kathryn's success and they spent most of the meal discussing the opening of the shop and the prospects of a prosperous trade. At the end of the meal, Thomasina took Agnes and Wuf out to the garden. Rawnose, who by his own admission had eaten and drunk *fit to burst,* sat bleary-eyed and smiling beatifically at Kathryn. She stared at the beggar's poor, disfigured face and wondered what crime had been so terrible to be punished by such mutilation.

'Are you happy, Rawnose?' Colum asked, refilling the beggar's wine cup.

'As a pig in muck,' Rawnose declared. 'And I've got news for you, Mistress.' He pushed his trencher and cup away and, imitating Colum, leaned his arms on the table. 'Servants chatter. And those from Talbot's household have strange stories to tell.'

'Such as what?' Kathryn asked.

'Well, Mistress Isabella is a virago and rules the household with an iron rod.'

'What else?'

'She nagged her husband.'

'Oh come, Rawnose!' Kathryn exclaimed.

'He was impotent,' Rawnose hastily added. 'Her dead husband, God rest him. One of the maids used to hear them quarrelling and Isabella moaned to good brother-in-law Robert that she found little satisfaction.'

'And Talbot's accident?' Kathryn asked.

Rawnose glanced away. 'Nothing much, but they don't believe the curse. They claim their mistress is happier as a widow than she was as a wife.'

'In which case,' Kathryn said and got to her feet, 'Irishman, you haven't drunk too much, have you?'

Colum groaned. 'Oh, no!'

'You are the King's Commissioner.' Kathryn leaned down, grinning at him. 'And an injustice has been done.'

'What?' Colum exclaimed, pushing his stool back. 'An old man has fallen downstairs and his young wife is happy to be a widow. Kathryn, it's not the first time I've heard such a story.'

Kathryn glanced quickly at Rawnose then back at Colum.

'I have an even better story to tell you,' she declared. 'The evening's fair and the walk will do you good.'

So, leaving Rawnose to feast himself even further, Kathryn shouted at Thomasina that they wouldn't be long and gently pushed the still protesting Colum out into Ottemelle Lane.

'This is none of my business!' Colum protested.

'Oh, Irishman.' Kathryn pointed at the blue sky now scored by the red-gold light of the setting sun. 'I thought you Celts were romantic. The evening is soft, the weather sweet, you have eaten and drunk well and you are escorting me through the streets of Canterbury.' She linked her arm through his and squeezed it gently. 'Aren't you happy, Irishman?'

Colum glowered down at her in mock anger.

'I should be toasting my toes in front of the fire and listening to Rawnose's stories.'

'That can be arranged,' Kathryn retorted. 'And I could ask another to escort me on an evening walk!'

Colum grinned and tapped her gently on the cheek. 'And I'd take his head, so tell me your story, woman!'

'I think Isabella Talbot murdered her husband.'

Colum stopped and gaped open-mouthed. 'Kathryn, we are going to walk into a powerful merchant's house and accuse his widow of murder? Can you prove it?'

'No.' Kathryn stared defiantly back. 'But I want to challenge her. I want her to realise that others may know the truth and that could be a beginning!'

Kathryn was still talking when they reached Talbot's house. Colum, though not happy, grudgingly conceded there was a case to answer. At first Kathryn thought Isabella would refuse to see her; Colum, however, wedged his foot in the door and loudly exclaimed that she would either see them now or be summoned to the Guildhall early on the morrow to answer certain matters. The servant ushered them into a small parlour where they waited until Isabella Talbot, followed by the ubiquitous Robert, swept into the room. Her face was a mask of fury.

'How dare you!' she began. 'How dare you come here, after taking the side of that filthy, old woman who murdered my husband with her evil magic and malevolent curses! I shall protest!'

'Oh, shut up!' Colum snapped: his gaze never left Isabella as he pointed at Robert. 'And you, sir, can stay where you are. Let me introduce myself, Mistress Talbot. I am Colum Murtagh, Royal Commissioner. Your husband died a dreadful death and for that I am very sorry. However, you have laid grave allegations against an old woman. You are correct: Mistress Swinbrooke may not have any powers to ask you questions, but I certainly have!'

Isabella gazed back, not one whit abashed.

'In which case, Master Murtagh, King's Commissioner,' she cooed mockingly, 'you must have your way in these matters, but when they are finished, I will still make my complaint!' She glanced malevolently at Kathryn.

'Good!' Colum clapped his hands together. 'In the meantime I wish to see all your household: apprentices, scullions, servants, kitchen maids. You have a hall?'

'Of course, farther down the gallery where the apprentices sleep.'

'Excellent, I'll see them there.'

'For what purpose?' Robert bleated.

'To ask them certain questions about the morning their master was killed.'

Isabella took a step forward. 'You have our sworn statement on that.'

'Aye.' Colum smiled grimly. 'Sworn statement indeed, but it is not the truth, Mistress Talbot, and perjury is an indictable offence. Now, do what I say!'

Isabella was about to argue, but thought better of it. She clawed at her black taffeta skirt, pouted and swept out of the room, snapping her fingers at Robert to follow. Colum watched her go.

'Chaucer says "Truth is a dangerous thing",' he remarked over his shoulder. 'I do hope, oh sharpest of physicians, that your suspicions are correct.'

'They are,' Kathryn replied confidently, sitting down on the window seat. 'Isabella Talbot is a murderess, a clever one, though on this occasion, too clever by half.'

They sat and waited for a while. At last a sour-faced housekeeper tapped on the door and told them all was ready. She led them down the ornately furnished passageway and into the small hall. Kathryn gazed appreciatively round at the polished wainscoting, which covered most of the wall, and the beautifully carved hearth with two mermaids supporting the marble mantel. All the furniture, cupboards, aumbries and chests were of brightly polished oak whilst fresh, green rushes covered the shining floorboards. At the far end, under a large rose window, was a long table with a slightly raised dais. In the middle of this stood a huge, silver salt-cellar in the shape of a tower. The servants had been gathered just below the dais, sitting on benches as if they were preparing to hear Mass. They turned as Kathryn came in.

'You may sit here, beside me,' Isabella Talbot declared, stepping elegantly onto the dais. She sat down in a throne-like chair, indicating two very small stools to her right.

Colum bowed. 'I think we'll stand.' Before Isabella or Robert, who was standing behind her, could object, Colum and Kathryn stood on the dais, the table behind them, and faced the assembled household.

The sleepy-eyed apprentices, maids and scullions watched them open-mouthed as if Kathryn and Colum were mummers or jugglers come for entertainment.

'I am sorry to disturb you,' Kathryn announced, 'but this is Colum Murtagh.'

'I have told them that already!' Isabella snapped.

'In which case,' Kathryn continued, 'I'll ask my questions.' She glanced at the apprentices. 'Who was responsible for the stalls outside your master's house the morning he died?'

A large, gangly youth raised his hand.

'I am the master apprentice, Mistress. We did nothing wrong that morning,' he explained in a rush of words, 'except . . .'

'Except what?' Kathryn asked.

'We had a peeing contest up the wall of the adjoining house.'

Kathryn glanced threateningly at Colum, daring him to laugh.

'We were seeing who could pee the highest,' the lad continued. 'But then we came back to the stalls. We finished bringing out the goods and arranging them there. There were some urchins around: the usual rogues trying to steal a buckle or one of the wallets. They buzz around like flies above a dung heap.'

'And they come every day?' Kathryn asked.

'Oh, yes,' the lad replied. 'They are like the weather, part of the trade. We were shooing them away when we heard the master yell and a terrible crashing from upstairs. I told the apprentices to stay there and came rushing in. Sir Peter was lying on the floor, his head strangely twisted.' He looked round at his companions. 'I knows he was dead. I said as much, didn't I?'

A chorus of assent greeted his words.

'And then what happened?' Colum asked.

'Oh, she, I mean my mistress, told me to go back and look after the stalls.'

Kathryn looked at the maids. 'Then what happened?'

'I can answer for them.' The sour-faced housekeeper spoke up from where she stood at the back, jangling her bunch of keys. 'That morning,' she declared pompously, walking towards the dais, 'Mistress set all the maids cleaning the kitchen and hall. We, too, heard the crashing on the stairs. I came out.' The woman's voice shook. 'The master was just lying there.'

'What happened then?' Colum asked.

'Well, Master Robert was in the hallway already. He ran when his brother fell. My mistress shooed all the maids away.'

'And?'

The housekeeper closed her eyes and jingled her keys.

'Master Robert stood in the hall and supervised some of the servants whilst my mistress went back upstairs to prepare the master's bed chamber. The corpse,' the woman's voice quavered, 'was taken there. I asked if I should accompany her.' The housekeeper glanced fleetingly at her mistress. 'But I was told to stay downstairs.'

'Thank you.' Kathryn looked over her shoulder at Isabella. 'We have finished.' She smiled.

They all waited in silence as the servants and apprentices, chattering quietly amongst themselves, filed out of the hall. Isabella rose from her chair and swept around the table to confront them.

'What is all this about? Why this constant questioning?' Her pretty face was mottled with fury, eyes venomous, her lips tight. Nevertheless Kathryn detected fear beneath the anger whilst kinsman Robert was looking longingly at the door, as if he desperately wished to be elsewhere.

'I'd like to go to the bed chamber,' Kathryn asked. 'I want to see it.'

'Why?' Isabella retorted.

'A few minutes,' Kathryn answered. 'That's all I ask, then we'll be gone.'

Isabella, breathing noisily, swept down the hall, and with Robert following behind, they clambered up the steep stairs. At the top Kathryn bent down to look at the newel post and then at the plaster on the other side, just above the floor.

'What is it?' Robert stuttered trying to look round Colum.

Isabella came swiftly back to the top of the stairs, fearful rather than angry. She opened her mouth to ask questions but then thought differently.

'I am waiting,' she muttered.

'Oh, yes, so you are.' Kathryn smiled up at her and followed her across the gallery into the opulently furnished master bedroom. The drapes round the great four-poster bed had been pulled aside and, without any invitation, Kathryn sat down on the edge of the bed.

'Your husband sat here, yes?'

Isabella, now playing nervously with a ring on her finger, nodded and glanced quickly at Robert. Colum stood by the door, watching Kathryn entice both of them into her web of questions.

'And where were you, Mistress?'

'I went across to the window and looked out.'

'Ah, yes, you saw the urchins attempting to filch things from the stalls?'

Isabella shrugged. Kathryn glanced at Robert who had now sat down in a high-backed chair: his face was pallid as he nervously chewed the corner of his mouth.

'And where were you, sir?'

'I was downstairs.'

'Where?'

'I, I can't remember . . .' he stuttered.

Kathryn rose to her feet. 'Everyone else can. Perhaps I should ask the servants?'

'I was in the hallway. Yes,' Robert stammered, 'I was preparing for . . .'

'Don't lie!' Kathryn walked over to the window. 'It's getting dark outside. But I can see the cobbles below.' She glanced at Isabella, now standing rigid as a statue. 'But I can't see your husband's stalls or where his apprentices would have stood. I can only do that by opening the casement and peering out. Yet, even if I did that, I would have to lean out far to see the stalls, never mind some quick-fingered urchins trying to filch your dead husband's goods.'

'What are you saying?' Isabella sat down on the top of a large open chest, trying to compose herself.

'What I am saying, Mistress,' Kathryn replied, 'is that you are a malicious and wicked woman who murdered her husband.'

Isabella kept her head down.

'You deliberately evicted Mathilda Sempler from her little cottage near the Stour. You knew what her reaction would be. She would curse, speak her mind, and with her reputation as a witch, it would be easy to cast her into the role of some malignant warlock conspiring against your husband's life.'

She glanced across at Colum who had now closed the bed chamber door and stood with his back to it. 'Mathilda Sempler,'

Kathryn continued, 'did not disappoint you. In the full view of the parish, she cursed your husband and sent the same malediction to this house. After that it was easy for you and your paramour Robert. Sir Peter, I suppose, had his usual routine and you had yours. On the morning he died, you ensured that the maids and the servants were kept below stairs: that's why Robert was standing in the hallway, making sure no one went upstairs. What you did, Mistress, was come upstairs and tie a piece of twine across the top, wrapping it round nails on the newel post and in the plaster on the wall opposite. Robert had probably put them there.'

Isabella lifted her face. 'Is that what you were looking for, woman?'

'Yes,' Kathryn answered. 'Oh, the nails have gone as has the piece of twine but not the holes. You set the trap and came in here. Your husband was already agitated and nervous. You looked through the window, exclaimed that thieves were pilfering his goods. Sir Peter, of course, rushes out. A heavily built man, he catches his foot in the clever snare you have set.' Kathryn paused. 'You went down first, didn't you?' she asked quickly. 'That would certainly remove any suspicion of foul play. But your husband was trapped. The stairs are high and steep. Down he goes, crashing and banging his head and neck against the wood till he smashes his head on the stone floor of the hall way. You hurry back, acting the distraught wife. Whilst your accomplice here tends to the corpse, you go back upstairs, cut the twine with a small knife you probably had in your purse. No one would notice. They'd see you pause, bend down but, there again, you are so overcome with grief, your moods and movements would be strange. Your husband's corpse is brought up and laid on the bed. Everyone goes downstairs, not noticing the innocuous small nails which you or Robert later remove.' Kathryn went over and looked out of the window. 'A clever murder. I really must thank Torquil the carpenter's wife.' She looked over her shoulder.

Isabella was glaring evilly at her whilst Robert sat, head in hands.

'The ways of the world are strange, Mistress Talbot. If I had not looked out of a carpenter's window earlier today, I would never have guessed.' Kathryn shrugged. 'The rest is merely surmise.'

Isabella sprang to her feet, but instead of approaching Kathryn, she went and leaned over and whispered quietly in Robert's ear. Then she turned, walking towards Kathryn like some angry cat.

'Mere surmise, Mistress Swinbrooke!' she spat. 'Your story is a failure. You have no evidence, no proof for these filthy allegations!'

Kathryn held her ground. Colum walked softly across, his hand dropping to the hilt of his dagger. Kathryn studied Isabella Talbot and wondered what could turn such a beautiful woman to murder.

'I have no evidence,' Kathryn declared. 'And now I am going to leave you.' She walked round Isabella and went towards the door which Colum opened.

'What will you do now?' Robert shouted anxiously.

Kathryn turned, trying to ignore the malicious smile on Isabella's face.

'What can I do? I can prove that Isabella could see nothing from that window. I can point to the nail holes in the plaster. I can reflect on how strange it was that, on that particular morning, no one was allowed to come upstairs or that you were hanging about in the hallway as if waiting for something to happen.' Kathryn pointed at Isabella. 'That murdering bitch is correct, it's all surmise.' Kathryn paused to secure the clasp on her cloak. 'Tomorrow morning I can go in front of the justices. I and Master Murtagh here will go on oath to reveal our suspicions. Mathilda Sempler may yet burn, but oh, Master Robert, how the tongues will clack. The servants will begin to remember certain items, happenings, occurrences, and the whispering will begin. At first a few murmurs but then it will grow into a roar: adulterers, fornicators, murderers, assassins! And what happens then, Master Robert, eh? Will the local priest refuse to give you the sacraments? Will people stand aside from you in the street, the church and the market place? Your apprentices will stand idle, your stalls unvisited, a slow malingering death.'

Colum walked across to where Isabella now stood beside Robert; just studying their faces he knew they were murderers.

'As God is my witness,' he murmured, thrusting his face only a few inches away from Isabella's. 'If Mathilda Sempler is not free by the time the market horn sounds tomorrow morning, I will go before the King's Justice and swear to what I have seen and heard this evening. Mistress Talbot, that is not a threat, it is my solemn promise!'

Kathryn and Colum went down the stairs and let themselves out into the darkening streets. Household lamps, lit and placed on the hooks above doors, bathed the narrow alley-ways in circles of light. The crowds had now disappeared, the shops closed, the stalls withdrawn. Even the great cathedral had shut its gates to pilgrims who now thronged into the taverns and alehouses. For a while Kathryn and Colum walked in silence. Then the Irishman ruefully began reflecting how the bitter rivalries and deadly jealousies of court were mirrored in the lives of ordinary citizens.

'So much hate,' he murmured, 'in someone so beautiful.' He linked his arm through that of Kathryn's. 'The Pardoner said the love of money is the root of all evil.'

Kathryn glanced up at him and smiled. 'I think you have chosen the wrong tale, Colum. The Nun's Priest spoke truth in his story about Chanticleer the cock; arrogance, rather than avarice, is the open wound festering in Mistress Talbot. Spoilt and pampered, Master Robert undoubtedly gave her what her husband was unable to. Sir Peter became an encumbrance, an obstacle to her own desires, so she cleverly removed him.' She sighed. 'But it's all conjecture, very little proof.'

'I don't know.' Colum squeezed her hand. 'Those two murderers will never forget that we know and the good Lord knows. Vengeance will follow them.' He donned his cloak against the cold night air. 'Aye,' he added softly. 'The Furies will come when they are alone at night and their lusts have been slaked.' He paused and winked down at Kathryn. 'Aided and helped, of course, by a little gossip and chatter.'

'Will Mathilda be freed?' Kathryn asked anxiously.

Colum walked on, pinching his nostrils at the sour smells from the heaps of refuse awaiting the dung-collectors in the morning.

'Oh, she'll be freed all right,' he replied. 'I wager Master Robert is already drafting a letter explaining to the justice how a terrible mistake has been made. How the allegations laid against an old woman are spurious. Mathilda will be released, she may even get her cottage back. Sweet Isabella is a cunning vixen. She would like people to gossip about her magnanimity and clemency.'

'And Tenebrae's death and that of Fronzac?' Kathryn asked.

Colum walked on for a while. 'Is there nothing?'

Kathryn shook her head. 'I cannot fathom it, Colum. Fronzac's death, yes. I am sure he went out to the hog pen, opened that gate and admitted the killer. I am also certain Fronzac had seen the Book of Shadows, hence his salacious remarks to young Louise. But, for the life of me, I cannot see how he murdered Tenebrae. There's something missing. It's like those tricks the mountebanks play in the market-place, sleights of hand, which you can only detect if you know what you are looking for.'

They entered Ottemelle Lane. Colum stopped and grasped both of Kathryn's hands, pulling her close to him. He leaned down and kissed her gently on each cheek.

'I didn't want to tell you,' he began, 'but Master Foliot has returned to London. He came out to Kingsmead and took two of the swiftest horses.'

Kathryn's heart skipped a beat. 'And?'

'By now,' Colum replied, 'he will be closeted with Her Grace the Queen. He will tell her the Book of Shadows has gone. Tenebrae is dead and there is no solution to the mystery.' Colum stared up between the houses at the sky. 'I know Woodville,' he continued meaningfully. 'Foliot will return. He may be back by to-morrow evening bringing tokens of the Queen's displeasure with him.'

Chapter 10

Once she was home, Kathryn closeted herself in the chancery office, ignoring Thomasina's chatter about what mischief Wuf had been up to. She then sat for at least an hour, scribbling down all she had learnt about the murders of Tenebrae and Fronzac. Colum came in to wish her good night. He received an absent-minded reply whilst Kathryn sifted the evidence she had collected.

'Nothing fits,' she murmured to herself. Fronzac was killed by one of the pilgrims: the dead clerk had undoubtedly read the Book of Shadows. Therefore Tenebrae must have been murdered by one of Sir Raymond's group, the Book of Shadows stolen, and Fronzac must have been involved in it. Kathryn conceded defeat and wearily climbed the stairs, still absorbed in the mystery. She undressed and slipped between the linen sheets. Sleep came fast, but her troubled mind soon plunged into a whirlpool of fitful nightmares from which she woke in a sweat. Kathryn sat up, staring into the darkness. Outside she heard the tap, tap of some beggar's cane as he made his way up Ottemelle Lane, followed by the cries of hunting cats and the lowful baying of a dog. Kathryn smoothed the blankets in front of her. Fully awake, her mind and body were still plagued by the nightmare and a deep feeling of unease. One conclusion she had reached before retiring was that Tenebrae was not only a professional warlock, but a most skilful blackmailer: one or more of Hetherington's company were in his pay. Kathryn eased herself down between the sheets.

'Brissot,' she whispered, recalling the physician's fat rubicund face. Brissot was Tenebrae's creature who, whatever he claimed, dug up the juicy morsels of his master. Kathryn's mind drifted back into sleep. Thomasina woke her the next morning, loudly complaining that patients were already arriving. Kathryn flew out of bed. She quickly dressed, rubbing a little rose oil into her hands and face and then, putting a wimple around her hair, hurried downstairs.

Colum had already left for Kingsmead.

'Just after dawn,' Thomasina loudly proclaimed.

Agnes was churning butter by the hearth whilst Thomasina was scowling into a small cask of homemade ale.

'It's gone sour!' She glared at Kathryn as if she held her mistress personally responsible. 'Ah well.' Thomasina picked the small tun up. 'It will make the flowers grow better.' She marched towards the kitchen door beyond which Kathryn could hear Wuf playing in the garden.

'There's oatmeal cakes and milk in the buttery,' Thomasina called over her shoulder. 'I told your patients to go for a walk. It will do them good, though they'll be back soon.'

Kathryn broke her fast quickly. Apart from a slight dryness in her mouth and acid at the back of her throat, the nightmare was behind her. However, she still felt uneasy about Brissot and also wondered how she could inveigle the taciturn Morel into answering her questions.

Kathryn had to put such problems aside as a stream of patients arrived seeking treatment. First came Edith and Eadwig, the tanner's twins, both suffering from bruises after playing in a nearby quarry. Kathryn carefully washed their skin and applied a concoction of Saint Johnswort over the dark purple bruises. Torquil the carpenter's wife entered, beaming from ear to ear, to announce her husband was now far from death's door. Loud in her praises of Kathryn, she brought a small stool, in part payment, she explained, for Kathryn's work and pains. Coniston, an officer from the castle garrison, arrived complaining of gout, his large right toe red and swollen. Kathryn lectured him on the dangers of too much claret and applied the juice of hyssop. Coniston also informed her that Mathilda Sempler had been freed from the castle gaol because, surprisingly enough, Isabella Talbot had totally withdrawn her allegations. Kathryn hid her smile as the soldier continued to praise Mistress Talbot's generosity in providing the old woman with a fresh dwelling just outside Westgate. Beatrice, Henry the sackmaker's daughter, and Alice, wife of Mollyns the baker, also called for potions. Alice complained of a bilious stomach but left happily enough after Kathryn had provided her with a jar of moonwort. Beatrice, clutching her stomach and not smelling too fragrant, complained of a flux of the bowels. Listening to the girl carefully, Kathryn suspected that this was the result of drinking freshly brewed ale. Kathryn gave her some mugwort and a few pithy words about taking more care about what she ate and drank. Others followed, most of them minor ailments.

The bells of Saint Mildred's were ringing for the mid-morning Angelus when Luberon appeared, huffing and puffing, his hands flapping.

'It's happened again!' he declared, sweeping into the kitchen.

Kathryn was outside washing her hands and telling Wuf not to climb the apple tree.

'What's happened?' she called, hearing Luberon's shout.

The little clerk waddled out into the garden, narrowing his eyes against the bright sunlight. Kathryn peered closely at his red-rimmed eyes.

'Simon, you should be careful. You slept well last night?'

Luberon's head went back. 'Like a little pig.'

'But you were reading?' Kathryn insisted.

Luberon looked down at his mud-stained boots.

'I told you before,' Kathryn said, steering him back into the kitchen. 'Your eyes are becoming weak, Simon. You should do two things. First, only read in good light, never by candle. And, secondly, go to London, buy a pair of eyeglasses.'

'I have seen them,' Luberon growled. 'Pieces of steel with glass in them. They slip on and off your nose.'

'They'll ease your sight,' Kathryn replied, gesturing at him to sit down.

'Well, never mind my eyes,' Luberon wheezed as he sat on the stool Torquil's wife had brought. It was a little lower than the rest, and Kathryn had to bite her lip to stop laughing. Luberon followed her gaze. 'Is this new?'

'Never mind that, Simon. What is the matter?'

'Brissot's dead!'

Kathryn closed her eyes and sat down.

'I expected it,' she murmured. 'How did it happen?'

'No one knows. This morning the pilgrims rose. They'd planned a second visit to the shrine. They broke their fast and noticed Brissot was missing. The landlord went up to his chamber and found him just inside the door to his room dead as a piece of mutton, the back of his head stoved in.' Luberon leaned forward and touched Kathryn's hand. 'How did you know, Mistress?'

'Never mind. Have you been there?' Kathryn asked. 'To the tavern?'

'Oh, no.'

Kathryn collected her cloak. 'Then now's the time.'

And shouting instructions to Thomasina, Kathryn and Luberon went into Ottemelle Lane.

'How did you know, Mistress?' the clerk repeated, coming up beside her.

Kathryn immediately pulled him into a doorway as a window

casement opened and the contents of a night-jar came splashing down.

'One thing follows another. Tenebrae is murdered and so is Fronzac: the prize is the Book of Shadows. In that damnable manuscript Tenebrae kept all his secrets, including the revelation that Brissot was, perhaps, a greater spy than he admitted to us yesterday.'

'So he had to die?' Luberon asked.

'Of course. What good was it if Master Brissot could return to London, knowing what Tenebrae had told him? Moreover,' she added, 'guilds are like enclosed communities, where loyalty is a paramount virtue and betrayal the worst crime.'

They continued on. When they reached the Kestrel, Kathryn decided to waste no time.

'This is bad for business,' the taverner wailed when he met them. 'Two deaths in one week, Mistress.'

'Nonsense!' Kathryn replied, as they went up the stairs and along the gallery. 'This is nothing to do with your cooking or your hospitality.'

The landlord paused, his hands on the latch of the door.

'Then what, Mistress?'

'You have a company of pilgrims below,' Kathryn said, leaning gently on the door post to recover her breath. 'One of them is an assassin with a murderous desire to keep certain secrets hidden.'

'Aye.' The landlord pushed the door open. 'And by their fruits, ye shall know them, or so the gospel says.' He waved towards the bed where Brissot's corpse had been decently arranged.

Kathryn went across and looked at the physician. He lay, his fat face now slack, the blood congealing at the back of his head, staining the sheets all around him. Kathryn felt the man's stiff hands and limbs and studied the face, liverish white in the poor light.

'Such a waste.'

'Why do you say that?' Luberon came up beside her.

'He was a good physician,' Kathryn replied. 'But, as Master Chaucer says, "The lure of gold will outweigh any love of physic". He was killed because of what he did as well as what he knew.' She turned to face the taverner. 'I see little point in questioning the pilgrims. Did you, or your servants, notice anything untoward?'

The taverner spread his hands. 'Last night my guests were coming and going; visiting this place or that; shopping in the city or sitting in the taproom,' his eyes fell away, 'complaining about you and the Irishman.'

'And nothing untoward happened?' Kathryn repeated. 'No visitor came?'

'None,' the taverner replied. 'The physician was with them, but after supper they went their different ways.'

'And you found the corpse?'

'Oh, yes. I knocked on the door this morning: there was no answer so I pressed down the latch and pushed, it would only open a little because the corpse was lying just inside.'

Kathryn thanked him. She walked across and studied the door carefully.

'Look, Simon.' She pointed to the small, red dots of dried blood splattered on the woodwork. 'Master taverner, show me how the corpse lay.'

The landlord, cursing under his breath, reluctantly obeyed. He lowered his bulk to the floor and lay across the threshold.

'Like this,' he said, looking over at Kathryn. 'His face was turned inwards.'

Kathryn thanked him. 'I wonder . . .' she whispered. She shook her head at Luberon not to ask any questions. Instead Kathryn went across and helped the taverner to his feet, slipping a coin into his calloused hand.

'Thank you.' She smiled. 'There's no need for you to stay, though we would like to, for a short while.'

The taverner agreed and fled from the chamber before Mistress could make any more strange demands on him.

'You were wondering, Mistress?' Simon spoke up.

Kathryn walked towards the door. 'Brissot was killed,' she explained, 'trying to leave the room. He must have been with the killer, discussing something. There may have been a disagreement. Brissot rises, going for the door, perhaps to go down to the taproom, to declare publicly something to his fellow pilgrims or even seek help from myself or Master Murtagh.' She looked over her shoulder. 'Brissot's hand was on the latch, his killer comes up behind him and gives him a terrible, death-dealing blow to the back of his head, splintering the skull, spattering the wood with small drops of blood. The assassin then steps over the corpse and leaves the room as quickly and as quietly as possible.'

Kathryn went back to the bed and gently turned the corpse over. She studied the jagged cut at the back of the head, long and deep.

'Now, what would make such a wound?'

'A sword?' Luberon offered, staring distastefully at the mangled remains of the back of Brissot's head.

'Or something like that,' Kathryn replied. 'There's no sign of any implement lying here whilst the murderer would scarcely walk out to the gallery with some club or stick dripping with blood and gore.' Kathryn examined the deep wound again. 'But a sword or the hilt of a dagger, both of which could be re-sheathed and hidden under a cloak?'

'Why don't we question the other pilgrims?'

'No.' Kathryn shook her head. 'What can they tell us? If any of them knew anything, the hue and cry would have already been raised. More important, they would question me, only to discover how little progress I have made. Master Colum's out at Kingsmead, Foliot has returned to London. Oh, yes.' She caught the anxious look in Luberon's eyes. 'And he'll be back breathing threats. Look, Simon,' Kathryn grabbed the little clerk's podgy hand, 'go downstairs, tell them nothing of what I have said to you, but see if you can glean anything.' She stared despairingly round the chamber. 'There appears to be no solution to this riddle. Keep those tired eyes of yours watchful,' she added. 'Look for anyone carrying a sword or dagger.'

Kathryn made her farewells and slipped out of the chamber. She went along the gallery, down the stairs and left the tavern before anyone could stop her.

Kathryn walked briskly, trying to ignore her panic. What could she do? Tenebrae was dead. Fronzac and Brissot had followed him to the grave. She had wondered about Morel and Foliot, yet neither of these had been seen near the tavern when the two pilgrims had died. Kathryn glimpsed a royal archer, his red, blue and gold tabard resplendent in the morning sunshine, probably some messenger from the court. She paused at a furrier's stall and pretended to examine a pair of gloves. Was that how it would happen, Kathryn wondered? Some messenger, hot-foot from London, carrying letters and warrants, ordering the pilgrims and, more important, Colum to present themselves at Westminster? And would Colum be allowed to return? Or would he be detained for weeks, perhaps months, before the Queen's anger had cooled? An apprentice boy grabbed the sleeve of her gown.

'A furred mantle, Mistress, a pelisse of squirrel fur perhaps?'

Kathryn shook her head and hurried on. Leaving Queningate Ward, Kathryn walked up Burghgate. The sun was hot on the wide, open thoroughfare, the noise dinned in her ears and the air was thick with a mixture of smells. Traders bawled and shouted; apprentices tried to pluck the sleeves of passersby, screaming:

'What do you lack? What do you lack?'

A crowd gathered round a dung-cart loudly protesting at the way the burly labourers were clearing the sewer, throwing the refuse onto the cart and not caring how many passersby they splattered. A dog, crushed by the cart, was being put out of its misery by a passing trader. Farther along, a group of tumblers and mountebanks had set up their own stall covered by a dirty linen sheet behind which, one of them bawled, was a woman with three legs and a child with a beard down to its navel. Kathryn smiled at the ingenuity of these strolling players. Next to them a chanteur, standing on a broken bucket, tried to tell the crowds that he had been in Byzantine when the city was taken by the Turks, who had taken his eyes and part of his genitals, which for a penny, he would reveal to any interested party. Two soldiers from the castle garrison shouted back abuse. In the middle of Burghgate a clerk from the cathedral stood on a cart. He was solemnly intoning the rite of excommunication against William Pettifer who had allowed his cattle to stray and feed in Christchurch Meadows.

'Cursed be in his sitting!' the clerk bellowed. Then he paused and rang his bell. 'Cursed be in his standing!' Again the bell rang. 'Cursed be in his eating and in his pissing!'

To the right of the clerk stood a white-garbed altar boy bearing a huge, purple candle whilst, on the left, a similarly dressed boy held up a book of The Gospels. The crowds ignored all this as they thronged round the stalls. Two whores came running through the market, screeching with laughter, their heads bald as pigeon eggs, their orange wigs clasped firmly in their hands. Behind them came the pursuing bailiffs, puce-faced and sweating, shouting, 'Make way! Make way!' The apprentices found this amusing and did everything they could to hinder the officials' progress.

Kathryn walked into the shade of a house, which ran along one side of Burghgate. The dust of the market-place stung her eyes; her mouth was dry and she felt a little light-headed from hunger. She glimpsed a water tippler; she was about to buy a stoup to cleanse her mouth, but saw the mucky froth on the edge of the bucket and walked on.

At the Bullstake she turned left into the Mercery and, for a while, sat on a plinth before Saint Andrew's church. Using the edge of her cloak, she wiped the sweat from her face and glanced quickly back at the way she had come. She was so sure she was being followed and wondered if it was one of the pilgrims. She felt better, rose and continued down Saint Margaret's Street. As she turned the corner of Ottemelle Lane, a tall, thickset figure lurched out of the mouth of an alley-way to block her path. Kathryn stepped back. The man pulled back his cowl and hood and Kathryn stared into Morel's white, podgy face and black pebble eyes.

'You startled me!' Kathryn exclaimed. 'For God's sake, man!'

'I am sorry.' Morel put his hand forward in a gesture of peace. 'Mistress, I am sorry.' His thick-lipped mouth went down at the corners as if he was about to cry. 'You've got to come!' he urged, his hand flailing the air.

'Why?' Kathryn asked. 'Where have I got to go?'

Morel smacked his lips and stared anxiously around. 'To the Master's house, the secrets . . .'

Kathryn's heart leapt. 'You have something to show me?'

Morel's fat face beamed with pleasure. 'Yes, I have. The Master would want it. You must come, now, before it is too late!'

'Mistress Kathryn! Mistress Kathryn!'

Morel turned quickly as Wuf came skipping up the street behind him. Morel's hand bunched into a fist. Kathryn hastened forward to meet Wuf. She seized the little boy's hands and stared into his excited face.

'What's the matter, lad?'

Wuf looked up at Morel and the smile faded from his face.

'I am just pleased to see you,' Wuf muttered, edging closer to hide from Morel's baleful gaze.

'Where are you going?' Kathryn asked.

'I am frightened,' Wuf whispered, peering up under his eyebrows.

'Don't be silly.' Kathryn cupped his little face in her hands. 'Why are you out of the house?'

Wuf blinked. 'Thomasina sent me for a message.'

'For what?'

Wuf's hand flew to his mouth. 'I have forgotten.' The little lad stared at Kathryn. 'Honestly she did but I have forgotten.'

'Then go back. Ask her again and tell her that I am going to Tenebrae's house.'

Wuf threw one dark look at Morel, turned and fled back down the lane.

'Mistress, we must go now,' Morel insisted. 'Where are your potions?'

Kathryn watched Wuf until he reached the house, then turned back.

'I don't need my medicines.' She tapped the side of her head playfully. 'Everything I have is here.'

Morel smiled and, spinning on his heel, walked back up the alley-way with Kathryn hurrying behind him. Despite his bulk, Morel moved with a speed that surprised Kathryn. By the time she reached the dead magus's house, she was breathless and the sweat prickled her face and neck. Kathryn wondered whether she was doing the right thing; Morel was now agitated. He fumbled with the keys, muttering, and Kathryn was sure he was mumbling some apology to his dead master. Then the door swung open and Morel virtually pushed her into the darkened hallway. The rotting stench made Kathryn gag and she pinched her nostrils.

'For God's sake, man!' she demanded. 'What is that?'

Morel just rushed past her, hastening up the stairs, gesturing at Kathryn to follow him. Kathryn did so, wiping the palms of her sweaty hands on the skirt of her dress. She found the smell growing stronger. She paused and made to turn, but Morel came down and grasped her by the wrist.

'You must come.'

And, whilst Kathryn covered her mouth with one hand, she was dragged up the remaining stairs and into the secret chamber.

'Stop!'

Kathryn leaned against the inside of the door and stared around. A few of the purple candles fixed in their black-painted sconces had been lit: these made the shadows dance. The centre of the room was shrouded in darkness, the stink of corruption was almost too much to bear. Kathryn grew accustomed to the poor light and peered at the dark shape which sat in a chair behind the table.

'What is this?'

Morel yanked her forward, slamming the door behind her. He almost ran her across the chamber until she bumped into the table. Kathryn felt unsteady. She gripped the edge of the wood, looked up and stared in horror at the now decaying corpse of the dead magus Tenebrae, seated in his chair. His body was still dressed in a grey sheet, his dome-like head lolling forward, mouth open, eyes half-closed, the white, podgy skin now a dirty white, like the underbelly of some landed fish. Kathryn steadied herself, staring at this ghoulish vision.

He's dead, she thought: rotten in life, rotten in death. Morel, standing at the side of the table, gazed expectantly at her.

'Is this what you want?' he gasped.

Breathing slowly, hoping her stomach would not betray her, Kathryn swallowed hard.

'When did you do this?'

Morel smiled like some little boy expecting a lavish reward.

'This morning,' he replied, his dull face now bright with excitement. 'Before dawn. I took the master's body from the grave.' He closed his eyes. 'Master always said he would come back within three days. That someone with the power would make his spirit return. I knew it had to be here.' He pointed at Kathryn. 'You have the power, Mistress. You know the words.'

Kathryn backed away from the table.

'You can do it!' Morel shouted triumphantly. 'You know the old ways!'

Kathryn kept slowly walking backwards. 'The door must be opened,' she said. 'If Tenebrae's spirit is to return, the door must be open to receive it.'

Morel looked askance at her. Kathryn's nerve broke. She turned and fled towards the door even as Morel came pounding behind her. Her hand was sweating and slipped on the latch; cursing she tried again. Morel was almost on her when she threw it open and flew down the stairs. Morel followed. Kathryn reached the bottom step. She glimpsed the overgrown garden through the half-open front door. She stumbled. Morel caught her by the cloak, yanking her back. Kathryn screamed. Closing her eyes, she flailed her hands, scratching and kicking as Morel tried to trap her in a bear-like hug. One of her nails must have caught his eye, and his grip loosened. Kathryn stumbled towards the door, but Morel jumped, knocking her to the ground, bruising her shoulder. Kathryn turned like a cat beneath him. She did not care what she did. Her knee came up, bruising Morel in the groin whilst Kathryn began to criss-cross his face in red cutting scars. She did not know what was more frightening, Morel's bulk pressing down on her or his dead blank eyes staring so fixedly at her, as if impervious to the pains she was inflicting. Kathryn fought desperately, fearful lest her strength ebb. At last Morel caught her hands, trapping her wrists. Kathryn tried to roll away, freeing her body from the crushing press. She heard a shout, glimpsed something falling, Morel grunted and rolled to one side.

Kathryn closed her eyes, trying to catch her breath even as Thomasina leaned down and, using every filthy word she knew, her old nurse pulled her up and out into the garden. Kathryn lay gasping and retching, not caring about the bramble trail which plucked at her dress. Thomasina grasped her face and pulled it round; even Kathryn was chilled by the fury in Thomasina's eyes.

'Compose yourself!' Thomasina snapped. 'Breathe easy and deep.'

And before Kathryn could stop her, Thomasina, still holding the stout cudgel, walked back into the hallway and gave the prostrate Morel another resounding whack on the back of his head.

Kathryn dragged herself to her feet and staggered towards the door.

'Leave him, Thomasina!'

The old nurse already had the cudgel raised.

'Stop it!' Kathryn shouted.

Thomasina looked strangely at her. Kathryn stretched her hands out.

'Thomasina.' The tears welled in her eyes. 'Leave him! Please!'

Thomasina sighed noisily, lowered her club, but kicked the prostrate man with the toe of her boot.

'I hope he's dead!'

Kathryn crouched down and felt the pulse in Morel's neck, which still beat strongly. Kathryn rose to her feet, clutching her chest.

'He'll have a very sore head, but he'll live.'

She glanced tearfully at Thomasina who came forward and embraced her, pushing her head on to her shoulder, stroking her hair.

'You've lost your veil,' she murmured.

Kathryn laughed. Thomasina pushed her away, her nose wrinkling in distaste.

'Faugh! That smell!' She looked back upstairs.

'Don't go up,' Kathryn warned. 'There's a corpse.'

And, sitting on the foot of the stairs, Kathryn described what had happened. Morel stirred so Thomasina sat down on top of him. Kathryn smiled and glanced at the rent fabric of her dress. Ah well, it had seen better days. Thomasina was now staring open-mouthed up the stairs. Kathryn leaned forward and tapped her gently under the chin.

'You'll catch flies!'

'A corpse,' Thomasina stuttered. 'This misbegotten knave dug up his master's corpse!' And, springing to her feet, Thomasina grabbed Morel by the scruff of his neck and dragged the still senseless man out into the garden. 'And what are you looking at?' Thomasina bellowed.

Kathryn hurried to the door. An astonished Bogbean now stood at the gate, staring at Thomasina as if she was some Medusa.

'Go and get the bailiffs!' Kathryn shouted. 'Quickly now, man! Say they are to come here.' Kathryn caught her breath. 'Say it's the King's business!'

'Well, go on!' Thomasina bawled.

Bogbean hurried off. Thomasina went across to the local ale-house and brought back a cup of wine, a small pitcher of water and a ragged, but clean cloth. Thomasina then fussed round Kathryn like a clucking hen. She made her sip the wine whilst she bathed her mistress's face and hands; she then reclaimed the veil from the stairs whilst still keeping a watchful eye on the unconscious Morel.

'Thank God for Wuf!' Thomasina breathed. 'I had sent him for some flour. He told me where you were going.' She stepped back. 'There! You are still a little pale and you'll have a slight bruise on your cheek, but otherwise, the Irishman will still be lecherous towards you.'

Kathryn smiled and sipped at the wine. The trembling had stopped but her shoulder and the small of her back felt stiff and bruised.

'You shouldn't have come here,' Thomasina snapped.

Kathryn shook her head. 'I would never have thought.'

Thomasina clucked in annoyance, but held her tongue as Bogbean came back with some of the bailiffs from the market. Kathryn introduced herself and mentioned Colum's name. Morel was pulled to his feet, his arms and ankles trussed whilst two of the bailiffs hurried upstairs. They came down a few minutes later, both green around the gills.

'We took a blanket from one of the beds and covered it,' the bailiff said. 'Satan's balls! What happened here, Mistress?'

Kathryn shook her head. 'Master Murtagh will inform the council,' she replied and pointed at Morel who was now coming to his senses, shaking his head and groaning as he was held fast between two of the bailiffs.

'Take him to the castle!' she ordered. 'Though God knows the man is more mad than evil.'

'And the corpse, Mistress?'

'Take it back to Saint Mary Bredman's,' Kathryn replied. 'And bury it deep.'

Chapter 11

Tenebrae's corpse was removed, the bailiffs carrying it gingerly out into the lane, complaining and cursing. Thomasina, at Kathryn's urging, accompanied her back into the house.

'You should go home,' Thomasina wailed. 'You need to wash, change and rest.'

'I need to get to the bottom of this mystery!' Kathryn said. 'So, Thomasina, let's snoop around before our masters at the Guildhall send their stewards to seal every room and lock the house.'

'Mistress?'

Half-way up the stairs, Kathryn turned and stared down at Bogbean.

'Mistress, can I help?'

Kathryn shook her head. 'No, Bogbean, you can't, though I thank you for what you have done.' She opened her purse and put two coins on the stairs beside her. 'Drink my health!'

She continued up into the chamber which still smelt foul and rank. Thomasina busied herself, opening the windows whilst Kathryn went back downstairs to close the door behind Bogbean. She returned to examine the lock on the inside of the door to Tenebrae's chamber.

'What's the mystery?' Thomasina asked.

Kathryn pointed to the lock. 'There's a keyhole on the outside as there are on the other two,' she remarked, pointing to the far end of the room. 'However, once Master Tenebrae was in the room only he could open the door.' She smiled at Thomasina. 'And that's the heart of this mystery. No one could get into this chamber, without Tenebrae's permission.'

Thomasina blew her cheeks out and dabbed at her brow.

'Faugh!' she breathed. 'The stench is still terrible.'

'Go down to the kitchen,' Kathryn urged. 'Find two rags and soak them in vinegar. They'll serve as nosegays.'

Thomasina obeyed, then came back. 'I also sprinkled on some herbs,' she said, giving one of the soaked rags to Kathryn.

'Well, search the other chambers. See what you can find.'

Thomasina, grumbling under her breath, waddled off.

'Nothing much,' Thomasina called up from the hallway. 'Bed chambers, a small parlour.'

'Keep looking,' Kathryn replied absent-mindedly, sniffing at the vinegar-soaked rag.

With the windows open, the room had lost some of its macabre atmosphere. Kathryn was surprised at how bare it was. A bench along one wall, but apart from the sombre tapestries, the only furnishings were Tenebrae's broad desk and the high-backed chair with the stool in front for his visitors. Kathryn went round the desk, carefully avoiding the chair where the corpse had been slumped. Morel had apparently kept everything orderly in expectation of his master's return. Kathryn opened a small casket but it only contained tarot cards, a small scroll of new parchment, a collection of quills and a pumice stone.

'There must be something.'

She went and examined the door through which Tenebrae's visitors left, then out into the small gallery and down the stairs. Still she could discover nothing. However, coming back upstairs, Kathryn found the smell of corruption so strong, she unshuttered the gallery window and pushed open the large casement. She stared down into the alley-way, her fingers gripping the sill. Curious at what she'd felt, Kathryn studied the sill more carefully and noticed two scuff marks on the wood, about fourteen to sixteen inches apart. Kathryn went back into the chamber, lit and brought back one of Tenebrae's candles. She held this against the wooden sill, carefully scrutinising the scuff marks. She blew the candle out, walked back into the chamber, easing her bruised shoulder and ruefully reflecting on the mistake she had made.

'Always remember, Swinbrooke,' she murmured, 'that pride comes before a fall and is the root of all evil. I should have been more careful in my examination.'

'You are talking to yourself.' Thomasina stood in the doorway.

'No, I am scolding myself,' Kathryn replied. 'I failed the first test of any physician. Examine the symptoms carefully and then draw your conclusions.' Kathryn struck her breast in mock contrition. '*Mea culpa, mea culpa*. I did not do that.'

'Well, it's all a mystery to me,' Thomasina grumbled, coming into the room. 'There's nothing here, Kathryn. Well, nothing remarkable: clothing, food in the buttery, bed drapes, furniture, mere bric-a-brac. I thought Tenebrae was a wealthy man.'

'Oh, he was,' Kathryn said. 'But he was also a mystery. I wager he has houses between here and London and keeps his valuables well hidden. Don't forget, Thomasina, witches and warlocks lead perilous lives. They never know when they might have to flee in the dead of night.'

'But what about books, muniments, manuscripts?' Thomasina persisted. 'Oh, I have found parchments and pens.'

'The same applies,' Kathryn retorted. 'The Book of Shadows was Tenebrae's great possession: he'd list everything there.'

Thomasina stared round the chamber. 'I wonder where he came from? I have lived in Canterbury for decades, Mistress. At one time Tenebrae wasn't here. Then, like black smoke, he swept in and everyone became aware of his presence.' She came over and looked sharply down at Kathryn. 'Tell me, Mistress, what mistake did you make?'

'I am going to find out,' Kathryn replied, getting to her feet. 'Thomasina, I want you to close and shutter all the windows.' She plucked the tinder from her purse and handed it over. 'Then light the torches and candles.'

'Oh, for pity's sake!' Thomasina shivered. 'This is an evil place, Mistress, and it's best if we were gone.'

However, one glance at Kathryn's determined face and Thomasina reluctantly obeyed. In a few minutes the chamber was transformed, the light and air shut out, the candles and torches flickering as if welcoming the return of the demons. Shadows danced, fire sputtered. Kathryn stared up at the Goat of Mendes painted on the ceiling.

'Truly the gateway to hell,' she murmured. 'But look around, Thomasina. See the pools of light created by the torches and candles. Now, tell me. If you wished to conceal a corpse without any visitor noticing it, where would you put it?'

Thomasina gazed round. 'I'd come in through the doorway,' she replied, 'and sit on the stool.' She pointed to the corner where the darkness was greatest, just inside the door. 'I'd place it there. No visitor would see it as they came in. They'd sit with their back to it, whilst Tenebrae talked to them, then they'd leave through the other door.'

'I agree,' Kathryn said, 'but let's see if our conclusion withstands scrutiny.'

She helped Thomasina open the shutters and placed the candles in the corner Thomasina had indicated; going down on her knees, Kathryn carefully examined the wooden floor-boards.

'Ah!' she exclaimed. 'And so we have it! Look, Thomasina.'

Kathryn moved a candle, allowing blobs of wax to fall beside the rusty-coloured stains she'd found there. Kathryn scraped these carefully with her finger-nail then went and stood by the window.

'Blood,' she declared.

'Whose?' Thomasina asked.

'Why, Master Tenebrae's.' Kathryn shook her head in disbelief. 'We now have all the pieces. But it's fitting them into place that counts.'

A short while later Kathryn and Thomasina left the magus's house and hurried back to Ottemelle Lane. Their arrival created more hubbub as Agnes and Wuf became alarmed and frightened at Kathryn's appearance. The bruise on her cheek was now coming through and Wuf excitedly pointed to the dirt and tears on Kathryn's dress.

'It's nothing,' Thomasina declared as Kathryn hurried upstairs. 'Just a witless, wicked man!'

'I'll kill him!' Wuf cried. 'I'll get my sword. It was the giant, wasn't it? The one I saw Kathryn talking to at the top of the lane?'

Once she was in her bed chamber, Kathryn crouched on the floor with her back to the door, crossing her arms about her body. For a while she just sat, eyes closed, rocking herself gently as she tried to clear her mind of Morel's violence. He hadn't really frightened her. She was bruised, a little fearful, but the incident had stirred other nightmares in her soul: her husband Alexander Wyville, drunken and slobbering, his arms flailing like a windmill as he used them to beat and hurl her about. Kathryn thought of her medicines, those potions which could be used to create sleep or calm the humours of the mind. She was tempted to go downstairs and seek some consolation there but she recalled the words of one of her father's friends, a venerable physician: 'Let fear purge itself: there's nothing a good bowl of claret and a sound night's sleep won't cure.'

Kathryn smiled. *'Medice, sane Teipsam,'* she whispered. 'Physician, heal thyself. This, Mistress Swinbrooke, won't do.'

She got to her feet, opened the door and went downstairs and out into the garden. She let Agnes and Wuf chatter around her as she filled two buckets of spring water from the butt and took them upstairs, reassuring Wuf that all was well.

'Can I get you some medicine for the bruise?' Wuf offered.

'In a while, master physician,' Kathryn replied.

Once she was back in her own chamber Kathryn stripped, washed herself carefully, towelled herself dry and dressed in her best finery. For a while she sat on the edge of her bed, combing and re-arranging her hair. She forgot about Morel, but concentrated on what she had discovered and the fresh conclusions she had drawn. Only then did she go downstairs and apply some witch hazel to the bruise on her face. Of course, when Colum returned, tousled and dirty from Kingsmead, Wuf screeched the news at him as soon as he was inside the door. The Irishman came storming into the kitchen. He gripped Kathryn by the shoulders.

'I'll hang the bastard!' he roared, his eyes searching Kathryn's face. He gently touched the skin just under the bruise. 'I'll take the bastard's head!'

'No, you won't, Colum. And let go of my shoulder. It's hurting enough!'

Colum stood back, pushing his thumbs into his belt, anxiously watching Kathryn.

'Assault! Attempted rape! These are hanging charges!'

'He's witless,' Kathryn retorted, 'and still under the evil influence of his dead master. Colum,' she pointed a finger, 'I want nothing done to him. No accidents and certainly no trial. The worst that should happen to him is a hospital for the witless or immurement in a religious house, which has the compassion to accept him.'

'And Tenebrae's death?' Colum asked. He gave a lopsided grin. 'You are cold and distant, Mistress. I know the signs: that clever brain of yours has been turning.'

'This clever brain of mine,' Kathryn said wearily, 'made a few mistakes, Irishman.' She beckoned to Colum to follow her down the passage to her writing-office where she closed the door behind them. 'For a while,' she began, pushing Colum into a chair and standing over him, 'I believed Tenebrae was murdered by Fronzac who then used the secrets he had learnt from the Book of Shadows to blackmail one of his fellow pilgrims. I was wrong. Tenebrae's death was much more subtle and the key to it is the order in which the pilgrims visited Tenebrae.' She searched amongst the scraps of parchment on her desk and plucked one up. 'They are as follows: Hetherington, Neverett, Condosti, Brissot, Fronzac, Greene and Dauncey. Now I have concentrated on how Tenebrae could be killed by one of these, that's where I made my mistake.'

'So, who murdered Tenebrae?' Colum asked.

'I still don't know who,' Kathryn replied. 'I know how.' She glimpsed the exasperation on Colum's face. 'I have no real proof, no hard evidence.' She leaned over, resting her hands on Colum's shoulders. 'I am tired, Irishman, and I am sore but I am more concerned about Foliot's return. He will come back here with royal serjeants and warrants. God knows whether I will see you again this side of Michaelmas!'

Colum smiled at her. 'You'd miss me, woman?'

'Aye,' Kathryn said, letting her hands drop. 'Though how much is my secret.' She held her hand up as Colum made to rise. 'No, Irishman, now is not the time for mooning or grabbing my hand.' She winked. 'There'll be time for that later. Now I am going to stay here and reflect on what we have learnt. I want to put the pieces together and try to reach some conclusion. If I can't, we will wait for Master Foliot. When do you think he'll return?'

Colum pulled a face. 'He probably left London late this morning, as it would take time to organise an escort and fresh horses. He'll be pounding on our door early tomorrow morning.'

'Sufficient time,' Kathryn replied. 'Now, only when I ask you, go out and find Rawnose. He is to go to Black Griffin Lane. Drag Bogbean from the alehouse in which he is hiding and tell him to wait outside Tenebrae's house. Then to the Guildhall, search out Master Luberon, he burns the candle late. Finally, go to the Kestrel tavern. Give our pilgrims short notice, but demand that they immediately accompany you to Tenebrae's house. Oh, and tell Luberon to bring one of his bailiffs and a rope ladder.'

'Why?'

'I'm going to stage my own mystery play,' Kathryn explained. 'My only doubt is what lines each player will be given.'

Colum got to his feet and opened the door. 'So, there'll be no supper tonight?'

'No.' Kathryn grinned over her shoulder as she sat down in the chair. 'Hunger will sharpen your wits.'

Kathryn picked up a quill and opened the ink-horn. Colum came back and swiftly put his hands over her eyes.

'Irishman!' Kathryn warned.

'You are lying.'

'What about?' Kathryn protested.

'The murderer,' Colum replied. 'You know who it is, don't you? Tell me and I'll take my hands away.'

Kathryn nodded. 'Yes,' she whispered. 'I think I do but you will have to wait.'

A few hours later as the great bells of the cathedral boomed out for Vespers, Kathryn and Thomasina entered Black Griffin Lane. They made their way across to the magus's house where the rest were assembled. Kathryn was confident she could prove who the assassin was: all that was left to do was to close the trap. Luberon and the Guildhall's bailiffs stood apart. Bogbean and Rawnose chattered in a corner of the garden. Each tried to tell the other news, neither of them really listening. The pilgrims clustered just in front of the doorway. Sir Raymond forced a smile as he glimpsed Kathryn, though his fleshy face was now sallow, his eyes red-rimmed. Thomas Greene looked nervous and kept plucking at a loose thread in his cloak. Dauncey stood resting on her cane, staring up at the darkening sky. Neverett and Louise whispered together; all looked fearful at being back so close to where their blackmailer had died.

'Is this really necessary?' Sir Raymond asked, coming forward. 'Mistress Kathryn, two of our comrades are dead. It is dangerous for us to stay here.' He licked his lips. 'London might be safer.'

'I won't keep you long.' Kathryn smiled. 'And I assure you when I have finished, all will become clear. Master Murtagh, are the doors open?'

Colum, a pair of saddle-bags slung over his shoulders, nodded. Kathryn steeled herself against the memories of what had happened earlier in the day as she led the group into the house and down to the stone-flagged kitchen. The air still smelt slightly sour even though Colum explained that, before she had arrived, he had sprinkled herbs and opened the windows. The rest of the pilgrims also commented on the stink. Kathryn refused to answer their whispered questions. She waited until they were gathered round the great oak table.

'On the morning Tenebrae died,' Kathryn began, addressing the pilgrims, 'all of you visited this house. Each went upstairs and into Tenebrae's chamber. Now the magus was a subtle and cunning man, who invited people into his web with a mixture of threats and blandishments. He could only prophesy the future because he had spies and confidants amongst you, as he had in other groups: those would provide him with tidbits of information, scraps of gossip that he could later use.' She paused to collect her thoughts, ignoring the black looks from Thomas Greene. 'At first,' Kathryn continued, 'you all came to Tenebrae in the hope of discovering what the future held for you but, in the end, you really had little choice, as Tenebrae discovered secrets about you, which he used for his own sinister purposes.'

'That's not true!' Thomas Greene shouted, half rising to his feet.

'Master Greene, it is the truth,' Kathryn retorted, 'so please sit down.'

She glanced across at Rawnose and Bogbean who stood open-mouthed, scarcely able to believe the drama that was now unfolding. Thomasina, who was sitting next to her, also bit back her questions. She had pestered Kathryn with a whole list of demands as they'd journeyed here, but Kathryn had remained silent. She had sat for hours in her writing-office, studying carefully the names of the pilgrims and the order in which they'd visited Tenebrae. Only Colum knew the conclusions she had reached. Kathryn now plucked this list from her wallet.

'I believe the order was as follows: Sir Raymond Hetherington, Richard Neverett, Louise Condosti, Charles Brissot, Anthony Fronzac, Thomas Greene and Dionysia Dauncey. So, Mistress Dauncey, I believe you were the last?'

'Yes, yes, I was. Why, what are you implying?'

'Nothing,' Kathryn declared, 'except that I want to repeat the events of that morning. Master bailiff, you will act the role of Tenebrae. Don't look so surprised, man, it's quite simple.' She glanced at Colum. 'Is everything ready?'

'Aye,' he replied. 'Mask, cloak, cowl and hood.'

'Good! Master Luberon, you will be Morel. Take our friend the bailiff up, dress him in the cloak laid out there, the candles and torches are lit. All he has to do is sit there: the pilgrims will come up to see you. They will sit for a few minutes. Once they leave through the door at the end of the far chamber, the bailiff will ring the bell on the desk and Luberon will send up the next person. Sir Raymond, you will go first, followed by Richard Neverett, Mistress Condosti, Dionysia Dauncey, Colum Murtagh, and Master Greene. Thomasina will end these proceedings.'

'This is nonsense!' Neverett exclaimed, springing to his feet.

'Sit down, sir!' Colum shouted.

'I promise you,' Kathryn declared softly, 'when I have finished, if this is still nonsense, you may leave Canterbury and go where you will. Master Bogbean, please take up your usual post at the back door of the house.'

Bogbean scuttled out as Luberon, shaking his head, led the equally puzzled bailiff up the stairs. They all waited in silence for a while. Kathryn stared at Thomas Greene, schooling her features, not wishing to give away what she had planned. At last the bell sounded and Luberon, now enjoying himself, came into the kitchen and beckoned Sir Raymond Hetherington who went up as quiet as a lamb. After a while the bell sounded again. Each pilgrim went up, whilst those who had been through the chamber, returned through the front door and quietly re-took their seats in the kitchen.

'Mistress Condosti,' Kathryn asked, 'was everything as you found it?'

The pale-faced woman nodded vigorously. 'It was eerie,' she replied. Her voice dropped to a whisper. 'Very much like the morning I last met Tenebrae.' She put her face in her hands and began to sob quietly.

Kathryn gazed compassionately at her and decided it was best to leave matters be. Mistress Dauncey left followed by Colum and Master Greene. At last the bell sounded for Thomasina, and Kathryn followed her out into the hallway.

'Go upstairs,' she whispered, 'and do exactly what you are told.'

Thomasina obeyed. Kathryn waited. The minutes seemed to drag, but at last Thomasina, beaming from ear to ear, came bustling in through the front door.

'It's done,' she whispered.

Kathryn raised a finger to her lips. 'Then keep your thoughts to yourself,' she ordered and grinned at the Irishman, who followed Thomasina in, his saddle-bags still flung over his shoulder. 'And the same goes for you, Master Murtagh!'

Finally, when everyone was back in the kitchen and the bell was rung again, Kathryn clapped her hands.

'Fine! Now, Master Luberon, bring the bailiff back down here and collect Bogbean from the rear door.'

Once the clerk had done this, Kathryn turned to the bailiff who was smiling in satisfaction at her.

'Well, sir?' Kathryn began. 'Did you act the part of the magus?'

'Of course he did!' Greene snapped. 'We all sat on that bloody stool and stared across at him, masked, cowled and hooded. It was like some childish game.'

'Is that what you saw, Master Greene?'

'Yes, it is!'

'No, it was not,' Kathryn replied. 'The person you saw was Master Murtagh.'

'But the bailiff spoke,' Greene exclaimed.

'From the depths of a cowl,' Colum interrupted. 'And behind a mask, it is easy to imitate another's voice.'

'But that's impossible.' Bogbean came forward, his face slack in amazement. 'I opened the door and let the Irishman out.'

'Of course you did,' Kathryn replied, 'but which direction did he take?'

'Well, he went round the corner and up the alley-way at the side of the house.'

'You mean the one that runs under the small window on the gallery near the stairs leading down?'

Bogbean blinked.

'What happened was this,' Colum declared. 'Sir Raymond Hetherington went up. He sat on a stool and left. Others followed. When it was my turn, I ordered the bailiff here to take off his hood, mask and cowl, and told him to sit quietly in the shadowy corner just inside the room where no one could see him. I left the chamber, keeping the door open.' He shrugged. 'I used a glove. I then went downstairs, out into the alley-way and climbed the rope ladder.'

'You see, before he left the house,' Kathryn explained, 'Colum had opened the shuttered window on the gallery and let down a rope ladder. Once he was out, he climbed back up this, removed the rope ladder, putting it back into his saddle-bags, closed the window and shutters and went back into the chamber. He then dressed and acted the part of the magus.'

'But I never saw him leave again,' Bogbean interrupted.

'Ah, that was due to me,' Thomasina intervened. 'When I went up, Colum told me what was happening. We then left the chamber, closing the door behind us. Colum re-opened the gallery window and went down the rope ladder. I loosened this and threw it down to him. I then closed the window shutters and went downstairs where you, Master Bogbean, saw me leave.'

'Something very similar,' Kathryn explained, 'happened the day Tenebrae was killed. I kept thinking only one pilgrim was involved in his murder but, of course, Mistress Dauncey, there were two, weren't there?'

The old widow sat, horrified, her fingers to her lips.

'On the day Tenebrae was killed,' Kathryn continued, 'things were a little different. The pilgrims weren't assembled here. They came to the house at different times, as arranged by Master Fronzac. You may recall the order. He followed Brissot, then came Master Greene and finally Mistress Dauncey. Now Fronzac and Dauncey had conspired to kill Tenebrae. Fronzac went upstairs, carrying his saddle-bags as Colum did. He entered the chamber and sat on the stool. Perhaps he said something to make Tenebrae laugh. The magus leans back, head slightly up. From beneath his cloak Fronzac brings out a small arbalest, the bolt is fired and Tenebrae dies. Now, Fronzac acts quickly. He strips the body of hood, cowl and mask and drags the corpse over to the same shadowy corner where you, master bailiff, sat. The body is hidden in the shadows. Fronzac hurries across the room. From the saddlebags he carries, he plucks out a small rope ladder, opens the gallery window and leaves the ladder hanging. He goes downstairs and Bogbean lets him out. Our good porter pays very little attention to which direction each pilgrim takes. Fronzac hurries round to the alley-way, it is narrow and dark, no one can see what is going on. Fronzac climbs the rope ladder, rolls it up and hides it, after securing the windows and shutters. He goes back into the room, as Colum did, for he'd kept the door open, then dresses the part of the magus.' Kathryn paused to clear her throat. 'Now this was the subtlety of their plot: it wouldn't take long. Greene has yet to arrive. Fronzac has used the time to set up his little sham whilst Morel will not let anyone up the stairs until that damnable bell is rung. By the time Master Greene entered the chamber,' Kathryn continued, 'everything was as it should be. He merely sees what he expects to see. Fronzac would help this along, imitating the magus's voice. I wager he was most pleasant to you, Master Greene?'

'Yes, he was,' the goldsmith interrupted. 'He consulted the Book of Shadows and tarot cards. He said that all would be well and that I was to invest in the King's new trading ventures with Burgundy.' Greene shook his head. 'The room was dark. Tenebrae's voice was sombre but I was more interested in what was being said. Only now, looking back . . .' he glanced nervously at Colum and fell silent.

'I know what you were going to say,' Kathryn intervened. 'Never once was any reference made to those matters you prefer to be kept hidden.'

'Aye,' Greene murmured, not raising his head. 'I was so pleased at what I learnt, I fair skipped from that chamber.'

'And then came Mistress Dauncey,' Kathryn continued. 'She joins her accomplice in the chamber. Fronzac quickly divests, pulls across Tenebrae's corpse, the cloak, cowl, hood and mask are put on again. They leave the chamber, the door closes, locking itself behind them. The shutters and windows are quickly opened, the rope ladder is once again used. Fronzac, clutching the precious Book of Shadows, goes down: Mistress Dauncey releases the rope ladder, secures the windows and shutters and goes down the stairs.' Kathryn glanced at Bogbean. 'You may remember what happened? Mistress Dauncey opened her purse to give you a coin but, in doing so, others fell to the ground. You dutifully scrambled about, collecting them for her?'

Bogbean, gaping, nodded.

'Just a little protection,' Kathryn added. 'A diversion to keep you occupied whilst her accomplice Fronzac left for Black Griffin Lane.'

'But the bell?' Luberon asked. 'Morel heard the bell sound as a sign that Tenebrae's last visitor had left.'

'Of course, I apologise,' Kathryn replied. 'Once Tenebrae was back in the chair, Fronzac or Mistress Dauncey rang the bell. Morel comes hastening upstairs to ask his master if he needs further refreshment. Fronzac, of course, replies: Morel, not expecting any different, returns whilst the two murderers, as I've described, make their escape.' Kathryn stared across at Dauncey, noticing how the rest of the pilgrims had begun to distance themselves from her. 'I've kept you over long,' Kathryn declared quietly. 'And that was my mistake. I was locked in a puzzle; I believed only one of you was guilty of Tenebrae's death until I examined the chamber upstairs. I discovered the blood specks where Tenebrae's corpse had been thrown and the faint marks on the wooden window-sill from which Fronzac made his escape by the rope ladder.' She paused. 'The rest was mere conjecture.' She glanced at Sir Raymond. 'It was Fronzac who arranged the visits to Tenebrae?'

'Of course, he was our clerk. But what was the purpose behind it all?'

'Tenebrae was a blackmailer. He knew about Mistress Dauncey's ailment and threatened her with public ridicule unless she married him.'

The widow put her face in her hands and began to sob softly.

'Tenebrae, marry Widow Dauncey, never!' Neverett exclaimed.

'Impossible!' Sir Raymond echoed.

'No, it's not.' Dauncey lowered her hands from her ravaged

face. 'What I suffered from is my own concern. Tenebrae sent me a letter threatening to make public mockery of what I am. He'd only keep silent in return for my hand in marriage.' She glanced pitifully at Kathryn. 'He wanted his hands on my wealth, my shops, my warehouses, my goods, my property. He made his claims,' she added bitterly, 'at a time when I had thought I had discovered happiness. Master Fronzac and I had become friends. Not lovers: there was no passion, no romance, but he offered a marriage of convenience, companionship, friendship.' She smoothed the top of the table with her long, bony fingers. 'Or so I thought. Mistress Swinbrooke is correct,' she continued. 'I confessed all to Fronzac and we devised a scheme to kill Tenebrae.' She smiled as if to herself. 'It would have worked. Fronzac even fashioned a wax image of the magus, drove a nail through it and left it in a public place.'

'Oh, yes,' Kathryn said. 'The magus died but his devilry didn't, you couldn't murder that!'

Chapter 12

Widow Dauncey glared at Kathryn, eyes glittering in her ravaged face.

'It was an act of God,' she declared hoarsely. 'Tenebrae was an evil, wicked man. He lured the bait, trapped me and there was no escape. If I had married him, he would have murdered me. He was steeped in wickedness.'

'But why Fronzac?' Hetherington asked.

'My second mistake,' Dauncey murmured. 'He left Tenebrae's house carrying the Book of Shadows. However, before he handed it over to me, he studied it carefully.' She laughed shortly. 'Besides the spells, incantations and maledictions, there's page after page of what Tenebrae knew, as well as where he had hidden his ill-gotten money. On the evening of the day Tenebrae died,' she continued, 'Fronzac gave the Book of Shadows to me. He said what he had learnt from it would provide him with enough wealth for the rest of his days.' She shook her head, tears brimming in her eyes. 'He also said he no longer wanted me. The next morning I had a few words with him. I begged him to reflect.'

'And he agreed to meet you behind the hog pen?' Kathryn intervened.

'Yes. I slipped out of the Kestrel and went down the alley-way. Fronzac opened the gate.' The widow looked so pained, Kathryn felt compassion for her. 'He began to laugh,' Dauncey said. 'He said he'd buy a tavern like the Kestrel. I was tired: tired of Tene-brae, tired of Fronzac, tired of myself. I picked up a piece of kin-dling, ran after him and hit him on the back of the head. It was done before I realised. I opened the gates of the hog pen, thrust his body through then fled.' She looked down at her hands. 'God knows what gave me the strength or courage? I just picked him up, dragging him along the ground. The hogs were milling about. They must have smelt the blood. I then fled. I went to the gold-smith's.' She glanced shrewdly at Kathryn. 'How did you know?'

'At first I didn't realise,' Kathryn confessed. 'However, once I deduced that Fronzac was involved in the murder, I knew he must have had an accomplice. It was either you or Greene, the last people to see Tenebrae. I then reflected on Fronzac's death and your story about visiting the goldsmith. I thought how strange that a member of the great goldsmith's guild of London should have gone to a Canterbury shop to buy her wedding ring. Secondly, if you'd bought the ring, why not take it back to the tavern with you to show your would-be husband? But, of course, you didn't. You knew Fronzac was dead even before you returned to the tavern. And so, Mistress Dauncey, being the ever-prudent merchant, you left the ring with Master Procklehurst.'

Dauncey laid her hands flat on the table. 'Something so small,' she muttered. She grimaced. 'Fronzac should not have mocked me.'

'And Brissot?' Colum asked.

Dauncey half smiled. 'My life was in tatters,' she replied. 'And Brissot was behind it. He was Tenebrae's little creature: his famil-iar, snouting in all our lives, looking for juicy morsels he could take back to his master. He suspected what I'd done. On the eve-ning I killed him, Brissot passed me on the stairs, his fat, greasy face wreathed in smiles. "You really are the widow woman," he whispered. "So you have lost two more husbands?" I glared back but I realised what he was saying. I wasn't free of Tenebrae yet. Late in the evening I took the walking stick from my room and went along the gallery and tapped on his door.' Dauncey rubbed the spittle from the corner of her mouth on the sleeve of her gown, her face now suffused with hate. 'It was never going to end,' she whispered. 'Never! Brissot was waiting for me. The way he opened the door, his fat face always servile and cringing.' She looked at Kathryn. 'You know what I did?'

'Yes,' Kathryn replied. 'Brissot's body was slumped against the door. At first I thought he had been running from his assassin, trying to escape but then I realised, ever servile, he'd usher you into his room and turn to close the door behind him.'

'He died differently from Fronzac,' Dauncey interrupted harshly. 'This time I planned it. Chattering away he was, even as he closed the door. I brought my walking cane back and swung it, one blow, that's all it took. Brissot was dead before he slid to the floor.' She paused and stared round the room. 'This is a house from hell. It should be burnt from cellar to attic so not one stone is left upon another. I hated Tenebrae. Before God I swear I wish I had never met him or, like the rest of you, been lured into his trap. Fronzac should not have mocked me . . . and Brissot. Well, he was Tenebrae's accomplice.'

Her companions stared horrified at her, unable to comprehend how this elegant, severe-looking widow could coldly perpetrate three murders.

'I wanted to be happy before I died,' Dauncey murmured. 'I pursued happiness throughout all my life, chasing moonbeams. That's what brought me to Tenebrae in the first place. I had fallen into a pit, getting ever deeper until I met Fronzac.'

Sir Raymond Hetherington got to his feet. 'I cannot listen to any more,' he declared, staring at Kathryn.

'That's right, Hetherington!' Dauncey snapped. 'Run like a greyhound, that's your way isn't it? Changing sides when it suits your whim.'

Hetherington ignored her. 'Master Murtagh, your business with us is finished?'

Colum nodded.

'In which case,' Hetherington picked up his cloak and, followed by the others, left the kitchen without a farewell or a by-your-leave.

Louise Condosti, however, turned in the doorway.

'The Book of Shadows?' she asked.

'Leave that to us,' Colum replied.

The young woman nodded and followed her companions out.

'You can all go,' Kathryn declared. 'Master Luberon, would you take the bailiff, Master Bogbean and Rawnose back to the Guildhall? They are to be rewarded for their services.' She glanced down at Dauncey. 'Send others here to help us.'

Luberon toyed with his belt. Kathryn glimpsed the hurt in his eyes.

'Don't worry, Simon,' she added softly. 'Tomorrow evening, come and share our supper. We shall tell you everything that happens.' Kathryn grasped Thomasina's arm. 'Go back to the house. Make sure all is well.'

Thomasina agreed and, followed by Luberon, the bailiff, Bogbean and Rawnose, whispering excitedly to each other, left the house.

Colum closed the door behind them and came back to stand over his prisoner.

'I know what you want, Irishman,' Dauncey said as she twisted a ring on one of her fingers. 'I know what both of you want.' The widow smiled as Colum sat down next to Kathryn. She leaned across the table, calm, composed, as if she was their friend discussing the everyday things of life. 'Let me see. What you are going to say: that I'll be taken to London and tried before King's

Bench in Westminster Hall. How the trial will not take long and I'll either hang at the Elms or burn in Smithfield. But,' she raised her hand, 'if I hand over the Book of Shadows then my punishment might not be so harsh.' She looked sharply at Kathryn. 'Do you think I'm evil, Mistress Swinbrooke?'

'No, Mistress Dauncey, just trapped, bleeding inside.'

Dauncey started as if she had not expected that reply.

'When I was a girl,' she whispered, 'I was beautiful. My father said I had a good head on my shoulders. Skilful with the abacus, clever with the ledgers.'

She put her face in her hands and began to sob. Kathryn and Colum sat and watched for a while. The widow composed herself, drying her tears with the back of her hand.

'I'll hang, won't I?'

Colum was about to reply.

'No, Irishman,' Dauncey turned her face away. 'I can't take assurances from another man.'

'Mistress Swinbrooke,' Colum intervened, 'cannot give any assurances. However, if the Book of Shadows is returned, the Queen will be merciful.'

'How merciful?' Dauncey asked, looking at Kathryn.

'Safety of life and limb,' Colum replied. 'Though your goods, houses and land will be seized.' He steeled himself to continue. 'What the judges call, "being hanged by the purse".'

'And I'll be turned out in my shift to fend for myself? An old, diseased beggar woman?' Dauncey sneered. 'The rope at the Elms or the fires of Smithfield do not seem so repulsive now.'

'There is more,' Kathryn spoke up. 'The King can show great clemency. Perhaps . . .' Kathryn paused as she heard the archer and bailiffs sent from the Guildhall hammering on the door.

Colum went to answer. Kathryn covered Dauncey's hand with her own. 'I'll make my own plea,' Kathryn whispered. 'There are religious houses, convents for ladies of quality.' Kathryn glanced away. 'Though, within their walls, it would be a living death.'

Dauncey's gaze held hers. 'I have your word on that?'

'You have my oath.'

Dauncey withdrew her hand and got to her feet, even as Colum, followed by the archers and bailiffs, came back into the kitchen. The widow woman looked over her shoulder and smiled at Kathryn.

'I feel no rancour. I trust a woman.' She held her wrists out and the archers placed the manacles around them.

'And the Book?' Kathryn asked.

Dauncey yanked her hands away, the chains clashing. She undid the small wallet, which hung from her belt. Kathryn came over and Dauncey thrust a key into her hand and squeezed a ring off her finger.

'Show this to Master Procklehurst, the goldsmith. Tell him the small sealed coffer now belongs to you. Sell the rings back to the goldsmith and give the money to the poor.' Dauncey laughed. 'After all, I am going to become one of them.' Dauncey then left the house, flanked by the bailiffs and archers.

'Let's leave here.' Kathryn picked up her cloak, aware of how quiet, almost oppressive, the house had become.

They left, Colum closing and locking the door behind them.

'Well?' Kathryn asked, gripping his arm as they walked into Black Griffin Lane. 'What will happen to her?'

Colum shrugged. 'It depends on the Queen. Don't forget, Kathryn, many will be glad Tenebrae's dead whilst the seizure of the Book of Shadows will be seen as a triumph. They won't care about Fronzac and Brissot whilst the forfeit of Dauncey's goods will gladden the hearts of the Exchequer.'

'I gave her my word,' Kathryn declared.

Colum smiled down at her. 'I thought you would. Oh, she'll be spared life and limb and live out her days in some comfortable convent high on the northern moors.'

'And the Book of Shadows?'

'We must seize it ourselves first,' Colum replied. 'Before Master Foliot returns. That book has cost lives. I want to see what secrets it holds.'

The goldsmith's shop was all boarded up, but Colum pounded on the door. The surly merchant, wrapped in his furred robe, a deep-bowled cup of claret in his hands, turned cringingly servile when Colum announced who he was. In the flickering light of the candles set around the counting-shop, Colum declared how Widow Dauncey had been arrested for murder and, showing the woman's ring, demanded the sealed casket.

'Most improper,' Procklehurst murmured.

'If you wish,' Colum retorted, 'I can return with some of the King's soldiers.'

Procklehurst fairly scuttled away. He returned, thrusting the casket into Colum's hands. The Irishman growled his thanks, then he and Kathryn left the shop and hurried through the now dark, deserted streets to Ottemelle Lane. Once inside her house, Kathryn placed the casket in her chancery office. Thankfully, Wuf was sleepy. Thomasina had already fed him whilst Kathryn quietly warned her nurse not to mention anything she had witnessed at Tenebrae's house. Once Agnes was in bed, Kathryn brought the casket into the kitchen. Colum unlocked the lid, drew out the calf-skin-covered book from the velvet pouch in which it had been sealed and laid it on the table. Kathryn took the gold ring lying at the bottom of the casket and handed that, as well as the one Dauncey had given her, to Thomasina.

'Tomorrow morning,' she said, 'take this down to Father Cuthbert at the Poor Priests Hospital. Tell him how, in the end, some good came out of Tenebrae's death.'

Colum had picked up the Book of Shadows and was already leafing through the crackling, yellowed parchment. He looked quizzically at Kathryn.

'Do you wish to read it?'

Kathryn shook her head. 'No. It's an evil book: it's best if only you read what's there. Then I cannot lie to Master Foliot on his return tomorrow.'

Colum pulled a stool up near the fire and studied the book, turning the pages over, now and again muttering or exclaiming to himself. Kathryn chose to ignore him. She helped Thomasina prepare the dough for baking; it kept her occupied and eased the soreness in her shoulder and the small of her back. She jumped, nearly dropping the bowl, at a pounding on the door. Surely not Foliot? she thought as Thomasina rushed to answer it. But it was only Mathilda Sempler who came hobbling down the passageway, her eyes bright, looking none the worse for wear after her ordeal. She bobbed a curtsey at Colum and thrust a small jar into Kathryn's hand.

'Some herbs,' she declared. 'Quite precious. Willowmarsh, to prevent nocturnal pollutions.'

Kathryn thanked her. 'There was no need, Mathilda.'

'There is every need,' the old woman exclaimed. 'Poor, old Mathilda, nearly dancing on the end of a rope or grilled on a skillet.' She sat down on a stool, moaning and groaning at her protesting joints.

Colum glanced up, but then returned to his reading. Thomasina came bustling in and, stooping down, gave the old woman a hug.

'A glass of wine, Mathilda,' she offered, 'to celebrate your release?'

'No, no. Old Mathilda has only come to say thank you.' Then, resting on her cane, she struggled to her feet. 'I shouldn't sit,' she said. 'I forget my years and the castle dungeon is an unhealthy place.'

She turned and before Kathryn could stop her, began to hobble down the passageway to the door.

'No, no, I won't stay,' Mathilda declared. Just before she reached the door, she glanced slyly back at the kitchen where

Thomasina was now busy and beckoned Kathryn closer. 'I have a new cottage,' she whispered. 'The Talbot woman has given Mathilda fresh lodgings, just beyond the London gate on the banks of the Stour.'

'So she should,' Kathryn replied, puzzled by Mathilda's attitude yet eager to return to find out what Colum had discovered. 'So she should. You were innocent.' Kathryn decided it was best not to tell the old woman about her confrontation with Isabella Talbot. She opened the door, but Mathilda didn't move. Kathryn shivered at the hard, cunning look in the old woman's eyes. 'You were innocent.'

Mathilda, resting on the cane, leaned forward on the balls of her feet.

'Was I?' she whispered.

Kathryn's mouth went dry: Mathilda's face didn't look so old any more. Her eyes were bright, the skin on her face now seemed soft and smooth.

'Was I? That bitch threw me out of my cottage so I wove dreams around her husband.' The old woman hobbled through the doorway then turned, one hand on the latch. 'You have a good heart, Kathryn Swinbrooke and goodness will follow you, but in the months ahead keep your ears sharp. I tell you this, by all the dark lords of the air, I have not yet finished with Mistress Isabella Talbot!'

Mathilda smiled as if to herself. And, before Kathryn could protest or plead with her to be wary, Mathilda Sempler walked away, her cane tapping like a drum beat on the cobbles of Ottemelle Lane.

Kathryn closed the door and went back along the passageway. She stopped half-way down to control the shiver caused by Sempler's words.

I am a physician, Kathryn thought, yet there are forces and humours and powers, which perhaps run through us all. She remembered Isabella Talbot's hateful face and knew that, in the months ahead, when that murderess least expected it, Mathilda Sempler would reap her own mysterious form of vengeance.

'Kathryn, come here, quickly!' Colum called.

She hurried into the kitchen. Colum was now seated at the table, holding the Book of Shadows in his hand.

'I have found it.'

'Colum, what is the matter?'

The Irishman's usually tanned, swarthy face was now pale and agitated.

'Tell me!'

Colum threw the book down. 'No wonder the Queen wanted this,' he declared, pushing it even further away with his fingers. 'Dauncey was correct: there's page after page of tittle-tattle and viperish gossip. Dark, malicious half-truths. Which great lord has been made a cuckold. The secrets of this bishop or that. Which baron or merchant secretly supported the House of Lancaster. There's enough in here to send people by the cartload to the gallows.'

Kathryn sat down. 'But there's more, isn't there?'

Colum glanced away. 'Yes, there is. According to Tenebrae, the King's marriage to Elizabeth Woodville is not valid because he was secretly affianced and betrothed to a woman called Eleanor Butler.'

Kathryn's fingers flew to her lips.

'If this became public knowledge,' Colum continued, 'then everything the House of York has struggled for in the recent, bloody civil war would be lost. The King's marriage would be declared bigamous, his son Edward illegitimate, with no right to succeed his father. If the King's enemies got hold of this, truth or not, the country would be torn by a fresh power struggle.' He leaned across the table. 'Kathryn,' he whispered. 'Just to know that could send us to the gallows.'

Kathryn stared down at the calfskin-bound book, fighting the urge to pluck it up and toss it into the fire.

'What will you do?'

'I am going to put it back in the coffer,' Colum declared, 'and say the key Dauncey gave me didn't fit. Let Foliot and the Queen do what they want with it.'

Colum snatched up the book and put it back into the coffer. He locked it and then, going out into the garden, threw the key with all his force into the darkness. He came back into the kitchen.

'Was there anything about my husband?' Kathryn asked.

Colum shook his head. 'No, there was not, Kathryn. Nothing about you or me or the little ones of the earth. Elizabeth Woodville will probably destroy it to protect her own secrets.' He glanced round the kitchen. 'And where's the lovely Thomasina?'

'I am in the buttery, Irishman, keeping an eye on you,' the old nurse bellowed back. 'As I always have and always will.'

Colum beckoned Kathryn over. 'It's finished, Kathryn. Mathilda Sempler is free. God will take care of Isabella Talbot, Dionysia Dauncey and the rest. Tomorrow, Foliot will return and I'll thrust that casket at him and he'll be out of our lives within the hour. The sun will rise, Wuf will be dancing in the garden, Thomasina is there to be teased and then there's you.' He grasped her hand, took her out into the garden and pointed up to the starlit sky. 'There's a poem,' he said. ' "Oh, come to Ireland fair, shall I . . ." ' Colum paused and put his arm round Kathryn's shoulder. 'Will you ever come to Ireland, Kathryn?'

Kathryn edged closer and nipped him playfully.

'Aye, and if I can't, Ireland will have to come to me!'

'Is that a promise?' Colum asked.

'Irishman, on this starlit night, that's the best you are going to get!'

Author's Note

The possibility that there was a secret marriage between Edward of York and Eleanor Butler is more than a possibility. Indeed, Edward's own brother, Richard of Gloucester, used this eleven years later when he usurped the throne. The Woodvilles, as a group, were robber barons of the first order: brilliant, brave, charismatic and totally ruthless. Henry VI's death in the Tower is as described in the novel while the main murder victim, Tenebrae, is modelled loosely on Bolingbroke, the great necromancer of fifteenth-century England.

—C.L. Grace